NINA

MICHAEL C KELLY

Enjoy!
Michael

MIGASHCO

Published by Migashco
Publisher's note: This is a work of fiction. Names, characters, businesses, places,
events, locales, and incidents are either the products of the author's imagination or
used in a fictitious manner. Any resemblance to actual persons, living or dead,
organizations, operating or not, or actual events is purely coincidental.

All errors or omissions are solely the responsibility of the author.
Printed and bound in Canada
ISBN: 978-1-9990253-5-9 (paperback)
ISBN: 978-1-9990253-6-6 (ePub)

To Gail

In moil and in soil
sunflowers brighten in rain,
in contentedness

Nina's Route

Finland
Shlisselburg
Estonia
Latvia
Lithuania
Minsk
Belarus
Russia
Gomel
Senkivka
Chernihiv
Poland
Bucha
Rivne
Kyiv
Ukraine
Medyka
Zhytomyr
Ostroh
Kaniv
Lviv
N
Slovakia
Moldova
Hungary
Romania

1

PRISONER OF WAR

March 2022

Kyiv was not the place he expected to be in, but there he was, his foot frozen in the slop of a thirty-centimetre gutter, his back pressed against one of the city's bullet-scarred buildings.

Wassil crushed his shoulders into the shuba stucco with enough force to break his skin. He was trying to shrink every millimetre of his profile to hide from the hobby killers, a term he used to describe snipers.

"What the hell does that mean?" Daniil once asked.

"Daniil, my good friend, you have never read the sniper magazines populating the death cultures in Asia and America? Based on what I've read, some snipers fervently sign-up to test their foes, show off their technologies, and count their kills. To me, that feels more like a sick hobby than conscription."

"That can't be true."

"No matter. All I know is we are mere soldiers duped into this war. But not them!"

Frozen to the stucco Wassil swept the area with his eyes. His colleagues were nowhere to be seen. In the confusion of their advance, he couldn't remember if he had become separated from them or the other way around. It didn't matter. They were ordered to keep moving forward or face a court-martial.

"And whatever happens, don't get caught," Wassil's sergeant told them before continuing. "They will scratch information out of you, then end you with the ferociousness of a European badger."

"That's not true," Wassil had rebutted. "They are our neighbours. We play together. We visit. Hell, we cottage in their hinterland and they in ours! These people are our friends."

"And that's what the other side says too, but we must try to kill each other because of one person." Daniil raised his hand to his chin pondering the sky for recollection. "How does the propaganda go?" After a second, he released his pose. "Ah yes, we have a duty to our motherland," he pronounced with state-accurate words and a tone of grinding sarcasm.

Wassil missed Daniil's optimistic worldview when they were Ukrainian, German, and English students at the Kharkiv National University.

"Where are you now, my friend?"

The ground rumbled when an exploding shell hit a high rise, spilling the contents of many apartments and kicking up a massive cloud of dust.

"Ouch!" Wassil instinctively sheltered himself by burying his head into his shoulders, scraping the back of his skull on the wall, and knocking his helmet off.

"Isn't that what the bible says," Wassil thought as he shook off the rubble from the side of the building. "Dust to dust! Everything is dust to dust. But why does it have to happen now, and at our instigation?"

Some of the debris wedged between his neck and the stucco wall.

"I've got to get out of here."

Wassil fixed his eyes on the alley across the street while he listened for any unusual sound that might put him in harm's way. Satisfied, he bent down to pick up his helmet. Then he heard the click.

"Where do you think you're going?" The words greeted him when he straightened up.

The face in front of him spoke in perfect Russian with one of those smiles you see on a tough guy tormenting a wimp. It was as if he were waiting for him.

"A stray like you ought to be home with his mother."

The Ukrainian wrapped his fingers around Wassil's neck to pull him around the corner of the building. A woman showed up from the shadows to cuff his arms behind his back. "This way, please." It was a solid but polite command.

No discussion happened after that. Wassil and a small group of his captors traipsed southwest ahead of the Russian advance. After an hour, they corrected to the West, toward Poland.

"Don't worry, my friend," the woman finally opened up in Ukrainian, "you will not be going to Poland. With luck, you will be going home to your mama."

"That would be nice."

Wassil imagined his mother at home telling her neighbours about how her son would soon be completing his compulsory service. No doubt she would be sharing her plans for his homecoming.

"We do not want you here, Russian," the Ukrainian woman continued, "and I'm sure you don't want to be here either, not under these circumstances."

"Wassil," he smiled.

"Wassil," she acknowledged.

The Ukrainians ushered Wassil into the back of a truck, then drove him out of Kyiv, through a countryside to another, smaller city. The truck stopped in front of a hotel. From the awning to the brass staircase, the building held on to its regal past, awaiting a proper shelling.

Inside and to the right of the stair, he could see an archway clawed into the panelling. It led to a basement bunker. The Ukrainian woman's gentle push in that direction caused a clumsy trip on the carpet edge, creating an illusion of violence. The woman reacted calmly to stabilize him.

"She knows we don't want to be here," Wassil told himself, "and my surrender, by military standards, seems to be playing out as a comedy." He sighed, half relieved, half embarrassed.

"Welcome," another Russian-speaking Ukrainian said in a tone indicating the beginning of a discussion. Wassil could tell by his demeanour that he was the bunker commander.

"Well, this feels familiar," Wassil said, "and not what I was told to expect." He remembered tasting chocolates over a cinnamon sprinkled espresso when vacationing in Lviv. He recalled the graciousness of that welcome. This greeting felt more like that than an arrest.

Then his sergeant's words clicked in his memory. "Expect cruelty!"

"Three things," the Commander continued. "First, would you like something to eat?"

"I would," Wassil was more cold than hungry, but the food was a start. "And please, I speak Ukrainian."

"We do not have much, except for what we've been able to salvage and what we've received from humanitarian agencies."

"As long as there is enough to go around." Wow! Wassil was happy he held onto his manners, even in war.

"Don't worry about that."

The Commander signalled with his left hand, and a young woman brought him a bowl of Borscht with a plate of boiled potatoes.

"And the second?" Wassil asked two bites into his meal.

"We need to take a look at those wounds of yours. Our medic will be along shortly, but before we do that ..."

The Ukrainian shifted his body and fumbled around in the pockets of his fatigues.

"Here it comes," Wassil said to himself. "The sergeant was right after all."

The Commander found what he was looking for, withdrew his hand and thrust the prize in Wassil's direction.

"Here is a cell phone," he said. "Please call your mother and let her know you are well."

2

NINA

"Oh, what now?"

This was the fourth interruption.

Nina anticipated a chatty evening with friends, a chance to show off her latest dress and share her homecoming plans, as long as she could prepare her meal. She knew the evening would be threatened by rumours about mother Russia's tense relationship with Ukraine. She was determined to have nothing to do with it.

"Thank goodness my son is coming home for good," she had told her first caller. "The joy of the event will easily overshadow the gossips."

"I wouldn't be too sure about that," the caller insisted.

Her second caller required calming.

"Ah, not to worry," Nina rationalized. "Russians and Americans! You know they're never happy unless they are pointing guns at someone. That doesn't mean they're going to start shooting. It's an old Cold War ploy."

"I think they already have," the second caller emphasized.

"There is no way to verify this," Nina had responded. "All internet connections and independent broadcasting stations have been shut down. You know this. I'm sure that keeps those foxy fakers out of our noses."

"That's what they want you to think."

Nina finally acquiesced by the third call. After listening to a lengthy account of atrocities, she interrupted her caller. "Why can't we leave those people alone?" She abruptly hung up before the caller could respond.

Nina set a dial to preheat the oven. She seasoned her roast and then began tying it in the pan. The phone rang again, mid knot.

"Okay, okay. I'm coming."

She never understood what it was about the ringing of a phone. "What power lies in a ring that causes people to instantly drop their tasks and run hell-bent on intercepting?" She plopped her untied roast into the pan and dashed for the receiver with the energy of a love-sick teenager.

"It better be good this time," she cursed.

Nina stopped before the phone to compose herself by collecting her damp apron to dry her hands. It didn't help. The receiver slipped from her wet grip.

"At this rate, I'll never get my roast in on time."

Nina could hear a faint voice on the floor.

"Mama! Are you all right?"

Nina broke into a wide smile.

It would be the last one for a long time.

"Wassil! My *lapooshychka*! How are you?"

"I am well, Mama. But I have something to tell you."

"Oh, good, because I have something to tell you too. I have already started preparing for your homecoming. I even called Olga to arrange for...."

"Mama! Quiet, please. I need you to listen."

Her smile disappeared.

"I am somewhere near the Polish border and am a prisoner of war."

"That can't be! Wassil, you little minx, you will be punished if you are playing a joke."

"No, Mama. Listen! I've been taken captive by the Ukrainians. So far, they are treating me well. They've provided food and medical attention."

"Medical? Are you all right?"

"I am. I have a small scratch on the back of my head."

"Then you are coming home? I want you here where you belong."

After a long pause, Wassil replied. "I'm not sure, but just know I love you, Mama."

Nina was not about to let her emotions take over.

"Is there a guard there now?"

"Yes, I am with the bunker Commander."

"Let me speak to the Ukrainian."

"It's okay, Madam. There is no need," Wassil replied, looking at the Commander as he spoke.

The Commander moved his face close to Wassil's ear with his arm out for the phone. "She wants to speak with me, doesn't she?"

"Yes."

"That's okay," The Commander whispered, "I would like to speak with her too."

Wassil surrendered the phone.

"Hello."

"Hello. You bastard! What have you done to my son?"

"My dear *Babushka*, I have done nothing, nor will I do anything. This man is a friend from another country. He's as much a victim of this war as I."

"There is no war!"

"Madam, you obviously have not heard the news. We are at war with your country. We do not want this man, your son, in harm's way any more than we want our sons. We would actually like him to go home and not come back."

"Then send him home."

"I wish we could, but to set him free could put him at risk. Russian artillery approaches and their shelling is often indiscriminate. Madam, I cannot guarantee your son's safety or ours."

"This is absurd. How do you propose I get my Wassil home?"

"The only way he'll return is if you come and get him. In the meantime, we will keep him here and respect the terms of the Geneva Convention. He will be safe, or as safe as the approaching Russians allow."

"If I come, how will I find him?"

"Madam, that invitation is clearly absurd. A poor joke at best. You cannot do that."

"Then why did you tell me I could? And one more thing, don't tell me what I can and cannot do."

"Apologies, Madam, but you would have to make your way to Kyiv, then head west to the city of Rivne."

"That is where you are now?"

"No! We are somewhere west of Kyiv, but I cannot say where exactly for security reasons."

"Fine. I'll come to Rivne."

"I suggest you don't. You will likely be killed, probably by your own people."

Nina ignored the warning.

"How do I find you in Rivne?"

"You don't. I cannot guarantee we'll be there. Remember? We are at war. We may have to move. We might be dead. It makes no sense for you to come looking for your dear Wassil."

Again, Nina ignored the warning.

"I'll ask again. Where will you be?"

"Like I said, I have no idea. At best, you can surrender to us when you get here, then ask to be taken to your son. Madam, it is a long shot."

It was one warning too many.

"Let me speak with Wassil."

"Right away!"

"He's right, Mama. Stay home. This will be over soon, and I will return then."

Nina heard the background whistle that usually hocked up an artillery shell. A moment later, the phone went dead.

"I must get to him."

3

LADIES' NIGHT

"What's that smell?"

"I don't know," Emma replied, shifting two freshly baked loaves to her left arm. "Maybe she's in trouble."

That was all Olga needed to hear. She shifted a bunch of yellow flowers to her left arm and opened the door with her right hand.

"Nina!" She called through the doorway.

There was no response.

"Nina!" Louder this time.

"Go away," came the response from the second floor.

Olga gave Emma the should-we-or-shouldn't-we look. No answer was needed.

"Nina," Olga cried out. "Are you all right." She and Emma plopped their gifts on the sofa and took the stairs two steps at a time.

"You heard me, go away."

At the top, they could hear a commotion from one of the rooms.

"Which border should I use to get to Ukraine?" Nina asked from the room as if she were carrying on with a conversation in progress.

They found Nina alone, dressed in denim jeans and wearing a red and black plaid shirt. Her arms were pressing down into the interior of a suitcase, frantically trying to fit a sweater.

"What are you talking about?" Emma asked.

Nina surveyed her room for something she might have forgotten.

"You heard me," she glanced at the women.

"Nina, you fool," Olga said, raising her voice, "I know you don't like to hear this, but there is a war. You can't go to Ukraine."

"Should it be our border?" Nina said with emphasis. "Or would I be better off going through Belarus or Poland?"

"Nina! You're scaring us."

"Of course, Poland would involve two awkward border crossings." Nina continued as if Olga and Emma were not in the room. "No, the most direct route is the best."

"What? Nina, you are mad."

Olga walked to Nina and took hold of her arms. The touch had an instant effect, with Nina's knee buckling. Emma rushed to help Olga catch her.

"My son." The words bubbled through a gush of tears.

"Rest awhile, Nina." Olga and Emma sat on either side of her, gently pushing her shoulders back. "Maybe you should lie down."

Nina resisted.

"My son."

"What are you talking about?" Olga pleaded. "What is wrong with your son?"

"He's with them."

"Who?"

"The Ukrainians."

"Is he all right?"

"I hope so, but he is in harm's way. I must get him and bring him home."

"You can't do that!"

"I will not lose another to a war," she screamed at Olga. "Besides, I can, and I will. The Ukrainian Commander said so himself."

Nina fell deeper into her despair as she recalled the face of her beloved husband. He had been taken in a Syrian war.

"The only people allowed in Ukraine are soldiers. Step within a meter of the border, and you are as good as dead."

"I will drive to the border anyway," Nina replied, "and make the crossing. I will go to Rivne."

"Rivne?"

"Yes, that is where I might be able to find my son."

"Might?"

"I know. Not much to go on, but I must take this first step."

"We will not allow it."

"Pardon me?" The threat snapped Nina into an argumentative tone. "You can do nothing. I will take advantage of the Ukrainian invitation and find my son. Do you understand?"

"We hear you, but we do not understand."

"Then that is your problem."

"Nina, listen to us. We will not allow you to leave this room."

"Bah! You cannot stop me."

"Hello!" Fresh words sounded up the stairs.

More women were arriving for ladies' night.

Olga raised her index finger to instruct Nina to stay put, then ran to the head of the stairwell.

"Stay there," she instructed the women below before running back to Nina's room.

"Come on, Emma, we must get the ladies out of here. Now!"

The women ran to the hall with Olga stopping at the bedroom door to issue Nina one last command. "Stay. We will be back."

Nina had already moved on.

"That's about it," she declared with a final survey of the empty room. "Except for this." Nina retrieved a Russian cross from above the headboard. The left side of Jesus's footrest had long broken off. The jagged edges at the breaking point were a tiny monument to her pain when she first heard of her husband's death. He had been atomized by an explosion in some Syrian port. "This I must do, Papa," she said to the cross before setting it atop a sweater and closing the suitcase.

❀

A small group of women responded the same way Olga and Emma did when they entered Nina's home. All were repulsed, and all dropped their flowers and baked goods on her sofa. None took to the upper floor because they had heard Nina, Olga and Emma arguing. Instead, they formed a line to listen from the base of the stairs.

"It's dumbfounding to be before a wall of the bewildered," Emma said to Olga as they descended to greet them. "Am I not right?"

The question barely left her lips before a barrage opened up.

"What's going on?" asked Arena, the nosiest woman in Shlisselburg.

"Yes, it's disgusting in here." The words quickly slipped off Galina's tongue. She could always find something negative to say about any situation.

"Is there a problem?" Natasha asked in the pensive tone of a rational.

"Cause if there is, I can call my husband." Sasha offered without knowing the scope of the matter.

Each reaction spoke to the character of the individuals, but collectively they were supportive at heart. These were Nina's friends.

Olga shook the group's questions off as she descended the stairs.

"Let me do the talking," she said to Emma on the way down. "You follow my lead."

"Right," Emma replied before disobeying. Being two steps higher than Olga gave her an emcee's advantage. "Quiet!" She roared over Olga's head.

Her shriek startled all, including Olga.

"Thank you, Emma," Olga nodded with polite condescension. "Now, everyone, listen to me. You probably wonder what is going on and why the horrid smell."

It was not a good way to begin.

"Yes, I thought we were here to party," Galina pouted.

"No, a celebration," Natasha chimed as if there were distinctions.

"Oh, that's right," came a reply from the back.

"Quiet!" Emma had found her forte.

"Nina is not well," Olga announced before lying. "She is in her bed, and we have arranged for a doctor to attend to her."

"Can we talk with her?"

"No. It would be best to let Nina rest."

"Is there anything we can do?"

"No. I mean, yes." Olga backtracked. "It would be useful if you pitched in to clean the kitchen and then collect your gifts. After that, please go home. I will keep you informed."

The women set about straightening the living room and cleaning the kitchen. Olga and Emma started for the stairs.

Their activities were interrupted by the sound of a roaring engine.

"Hey! Look here," Sasha announced, pointing out the living room window.

"Who is that?" The slightly nearsighted Natasha asked.

"It's Nina."

All eyes rounded on Olga and Emma.

4

PETER THE NOT SO GREAT

Nina said goodbye to the rearview mirror. She could see Sasha pointing, her friends gathering at the window before turning away, no doubt looking for an account from Olga and Emma. This would be how she would remember them, collectively concerned.

"There is a time for friends and a time for family," Nina shook off the sentiment.

Ahead was a different story. Nina could envision her son and hoped the Ukrainians were keeping him safe. She knew that a vast, hostile land lay between her and him. It would take time to traverse.

"But how much time," Nina said to herself. "I will need to collect my thoughts and make a plan."

Nina continued west to the Oreshek Fortress, then turned south along the Neva River, past the statue of Peter The Great. She recalled a community discussion about planting a formal flower garden around its base.

"Peter. Humph!" She blurted. "He doesn't need flowers. He is like all national fathers, either a libidinous drunk, an enslaver, or a wimp who can't take a bit of criticism without having people humiliated, or worse, brutally tortured to death. He is not so great and does not deserve a garden!"

She took a contemptuous peek at the statue through her rearview mirror. "I leave you to the artwork of my dear shore-birds and pigeons."

Nina drove an obvious route for anyone looking to get out of the town, and she knew one of her friends might give chase. In case, she pulled off the main road, down a side street and parked in a cul-de-sac.

She called up Google maps to outline the route, gauge the distance and determine the time she needed to travel. There were three routes, one through Russia and two through Belarus. The most direct route was thirteen hundred kilome-tres and took her through the heart of Belarus. For that, she would need eighteen hours.

"Belarus it is," she said, satisfied, "which means I will have to contend with two border crossings."

The thought of being detained caused her a moment's panic. How would she deal with officials, and how much extra time would that add to the trip?

"I do not know," she threw her hands up, "and won't until I get there. All I know for now is that I can be arbitrarily pulled over there just as much as here."

She pulled out of the cul-de-sac, onto the main road, and then into a gas station. She topped the tank on her Largus. In the back, she had four five-litre containers of washing bleach. She quietly dumped their contents into a nearby grate, rinsed them in the station washroom, then filled them with gas. The range on the Largus was enough to take her halfway, but she thought the extra gas might be a good idea. She determined to refill her tank at every opportunity.

Nina dropped money on the counter. "For the gas and a road map," she said. "Oh, and I'll take three bags of these cucumber chips."

"I saw you," the attendant said over his reading glasses while taking her money and opening his till.

"Oh?"

"Yes. Do you not understand the environmental damage you will have done by pouring bleach into mother Russia's water table? I should report this."

"Suit yourself," Nina said.

She could tell the attendant was surprised by her lack of concern.

"I'll tell you what," he offered. "For 300 rubles, I will not report you."

"No, thank you."

Nina snatched her change and left. She could hear him yelling threats as the station door closed, but she was not interested. There was a long drive ahead, and this guy would likely be the least of her troubles.

Nina pulled out of the station and continued south into Russia's western low lands.

5

LIDIYA

Wassil did not like that his conversation ended abruptly.

"Those damn bombs."

He wasn't worried about his mother's health. He just did not want her to fret.

"Wassil?"

Something was reassuring in the tone of his name, something soothing. "Probably a ploy to lead me into a false sense of security," he thought.

"Yes?"

It was the woman who cuffed him.

"The medic has arrived," she announced, "and would like to examine your injuries. It shouldn't take long."

"I don't need medical attention," Wassil responded.

"But what harm will it do?" She asked, bending around him to reach for his wrists. At first, Wassil thought she was checking his cuffs. Then he heard the click.

"What are you doing?"

"I'm freeing your hands. The cuffs will get in the way of the Doctor."

Wassil thought this an odd behaviour. Prisoners were to be kept permanently secured.

"There," she announced as she stepped away from Wassil. "She should be along momentarily.

"I am not worried." Wassil rubbed his wrists. "It's not like I have anything to do."

The woman stayed to guard him.

Wassil thought it might be a good idea to start a conversation.

"What is your name?"

"Lidiya."

"It is a beautiful name."

"Thank you. It actually means beautiful. The name was chosen by my father. Apparently, he told my mother they were off to a good start with such a beautiful child. So, that makes me beautiful and the oldest in our family, or what's left of it." What started out as an attempt at humour unravelled with the last words in her sentence.

"And it is true," Wassil tried to restore the mood.

"What?" Lidiya asked while smearing a tear away from her eye with her thumb.

"Your name, it suits you."

"Oh!" Lidiya ignored the compliment. "I thought you knew something about my family."

"Not likely," Wassil replied. "I'm not entirely clear on my status, let alone yours."

The conversation was getting awkward.

Lidiya walked to the end of the corridor to see what was keeping the Doctor.

"You don't think she'll try and come here, do you?" Lidiya asked when she returned.

"Who?"

"Your mother."

"I hope not. It is too dangerous, and there are a lot of

lunatics out there."

"Do you include yourself in that lot?"

"*Bozhe moi*, no. I thought I was finishing my compulsory service. We were on our final military exercise and looking forward to going home. I turned 27 last Monday, so they can't conscript me again."

"Well, happy birthday. At least you're still intact."

"That is true. I am so sorry for what we have done to you and your family."

"Treasonous words, wouldn't you say?"

"For a puffed-up dictator perhaps, but not in the eyes of ordinary people like you and I."

"Puffed up?" Lidiya had one eyebrow raised.

Wassil could see the nickname piqued her curiosity.

"Yes, have you not seen the photographs of these people? Their faces are puffed with injections of American toxins. It's supposed to make them look beautiful, manly or whatever. All they do is give comic expression to already swollen egos."

Lidiya registered the contempt in Wassil's voice but did not get a chance to suggest the puffiness might be due to photo manipulations.

"Who do we have here?" The Doctor stared into Wassil's eyes.

"Wassil," Lidiya responded in as officious a voice as she could muster. "He was found wandering alone in Kyiv."

"And why is this man not cuffed?"

"I thought it best to have his hands free, so you could do a thorough examination."

"And you are a medical practitioner yourself?" the Doctor asked Lidiya.

"A nurse."

"I thought so. And one who is not yet used to the idea we are at war."

6

MINSK

"My mirror would be destroyed if I could wear something out by simply looking at it." Nina caught herself drifting onto the wrong side of the highway again. "I'd best keep my eyes on the road ahead before I kill someone."

She took one more look into the mirror to confirm she was not being followed, then jostled herself to arrange her clothes for comfort. More distracted driving.

"Besides, why keep looking? I'll bet the ladies reported me, and the officials decided I was a fool. They probably think I am too much of a bother to retrieve. Or at least I hope so."

Three hours into the trip, she stopped to refill her tank, grab a few extra snacks, and use the washroom facilities.

Six hours later, she approached what she thought would be her first challenge – the blue Republic of Belarus sign stood alone at the side of the highway.

"What? No border station?"

Then she remembered. "Of course! There are no customs or duty checks between our two countries. What did the officials call it? Ah yes, the Union State Treaty of 1999."

The treaty never impressed Nina. She never thought of Belarus as a separate country.

"They are our lap dog," she thought, "so this should be easy. It'll be like visiting my neighbour."

The thought gave her pause. "Then again, visiting anyone in Ukraine ought to be like visiting a neighbour." She remembered trips to Lviv with Wassil and how they enjoyed meals at the Grand Hotel. "It used to be."

Five hours later, at Minsk, she pulled into another gas station for another break and fuel. The attendant spoke to her in Belarusian.

"I am sorry, Sir. I do not understand."

The attendant repeated himself with a forced smile and eyes averted. Nina knew Russian was also spoken in Belarus and was surprised the attendant hadn't mastered it.

"You are a person who works with the public, and you don't speak Russian?"

The man forced another smile while concentrating on some imaginary problem with the cash register.

"He says that you are far from home, given our circumstances."

Nina hadn't noticed the man behind her. He was stalky with slick black hair and matching eyes that bulged to the threshold of a pop. His grey suit looked too formal for someone loitering in the recesses of a gas station.

"What circumstances?"

"Madam!" His rigid bow felt more menacing than polite. "Unless you are a complete fool, it is hard to ignore that we are at war."

"We? You are Belarusian, are you not."

The man ignored her comment. "I suspect the attendant is more interested in where you are going than anything else."

"He is, is he?"

"Yes, I'm sure it is nothing more than curiosity."

"Then let him be curious," she replied.

Anger began to brew under Nina's skin. "It is you who are curious, and if you must know, I am a nurse, uh, a field nurse, to be more specific. I am on my way to attend to our wounded."

"In a private car?"

"Yes."

"That is odd, don't you think?"

Nina could ignore the conversation and be on her way, but this was her chance to prepare a convincing story before arriving at the border.

"It is, except circumstances caused me to be late for our departure. I am trying to catch up."

"To where?"

"Ukraine."

"Then I am afraid you will be disappointed."

"Why?"

"Because the border has been completely sealed. It is blocked by military equipment that has probably chewed up the roads. Your little Largus will not be able to handle the route."

"I will make do."

"Not possible. But let me help you."

"How?"

"Madam," the man said, "if you wish to continue, you will have to drive west to Checkpoint Senkivka. That is where the countries of Belarus, your motherland and Ukraine meet."

"So I can't go south?"

"As I said, it is physically impossible. The main roads are blocked, and all detours heavily guarded."

"Then I guess I have no choice."

Nina collected her change from the counter and headed to the exit.

"Oh! And Madam! One last thing."

"Yes?" She asked, her hand holding the station door open.

"When you get there, you will be questioned. You had better be telling the truth."

Nina sniggered at him, crossed the lot, and got into her car. She grabbed her map from the passenger seat.

"*Dermo*! This will add six hours to my trip."

Nina ignored the creepy station man's advice and turned south on the P23. Three kilometres later, she was waved over at a checkpoint by a man in a vivid khaki uniform.

"Less suited for battle and more for a parade," she thought.

"Where are you going?" The sentry asked.

"I am a nurse and on my way to help our wounded soldiers."

"How nice," the sentry said dispassionately, taking a single step back from the vehicle. "Now get out of the car, please."

Nina tried pleading.

"But I must get there soon. There is no time to lose. Our citizens are dying."

"Lady, they are your citizens, not ours. Please step out of the car and present your papers."

Nina complied. "I have to get my passport out of my suitcase in the back. Is that okay?"

"It is."

The sentry stood behind and to the side as Nina opened the hatch. He eyed the contents but didn't appear to be interested in investigating for weapons or contraband.

"I do not know your plan, but we will not let anyone cross our border." He whispered to her. "I'm sure you can appreciate the political repercussions. If you wish to go to Ukraine, you must enter through Russia at Senkivka."

Nina handed him the papers, and he gave them a superficial glance.

"I will have to travel east?" she protested. "That will add an additional five hours to the border."

"Likely more than that," he replied as he closed her passport and handed it to her. When she gripped it, he held on.

"Now," he asked, tugging the passport, "why would an old woman, driving a late modelled vehicle, think she could drive through a war-torn zone as if on a weekend holiday?"

"I told you. I am a nurse."

"Sorry, but I don't buy that. I'm sure your country folk have enough nurses already."

"But..."

"My *babushka*," he interrupted, "there is no other explanation. The best place for a Russian woman in a late-modelled vehicle is in her hometown. You should be as far away from our southern brothers and sisters as possible. So, I'm going to tell you this only once and for your own good. Turn this vehicle around and return home."

He gave Nina a depressed grin that betrayed how he felt.

Nina mirrored the smile, returned to her car and reluctantly drove toward Minsk.

7

SENKIVKA

"The gas station man must have been telling the truth," she thought as she turned right onto the ramp that connected her to the M5. This would take her to the P124 and checkpoint Senkivka.

Three hours passed before Nina began to notice the presence of military vehicles, mostly covered under shade trees. Caterpillar treads peaked from under their tarps like the leggings of a dancehall girl.

Small groups of soldiers could be seen ambling about at the side of the road or huddled around open fires, smoking cigarettes. All stared at her as she passed. There was no questioning in their eyes. None of them looked like they wanted to be there.

For the first time, she began to feel uncomfortable.

"At least no one is stopping me," she said.

Noticing military equipment was one thing. Realizing the diminishing presence of public washroom facilities was a far more significant concern. Nina had to resort to using a stand of vegetation as a bathroom facility at one point.

The M5 turned into the M10 at Gomel. "I have only seventy-five more kilometres to travel," she said optimistically, "so another hour."

The optimism evaporated when the M10 turned into the P124. Military vehicles formed in front of her, all crawling along the same lane and in the same direction. Nina's discomfort transformed into a combination of anxiety and impatience.

"I am close and conspicuous," she realized. "My Largus is the only private vehicle on the road." Every other vehicle was painted in military colours.

At the Grenzkontrollstelle Triangle, she was forced to turn left, officially into Russian territory. She could then turn right to cross into Ukraine on the P13.

"I see what they are doing," she said aloud. "They are forcing vehicles to enter Ukraine only from Russia. Someone did not want the Belarusians involved."

A few hundred meters later, concrete barriers forced her into Checkpoint Senkivka.

Nina expected to be challenged.

"This is it," she said as she rolled down her window.

"Wait, wait, wait," she could hear someone yelling like a director dealing with an off-script actor. "This will not do. Who is this person?"

Her eyes locked on a Russian officer pointing at her car while beckoning an underling. A moment later, he gave up.

"Hey, you," he pointed at Nina. "Pull over here."

Nina complied.

"Where do you think you are going?"

Nina reprised her story. "I am a nurse on my way to help our comrades in arms."

"You're a little old and fancy for that, are you not?"

Usually, Nina would be offended.

"Look. I am late, and my personal car was all I could muster to catch up."

"Sure it was. And the real reason for your visit?"

"I told you. I am to help our brothers and sisters in the special military operation."

"No, you aren't." His harsh response led to a plea. "Madam, please! I have a lot of traffic to move, and you are in my way. Please go home."

Nina mustered as much fake patriotism as she could. "I understand, and just so you know, I would sooner die than return."

"Madam, you sound like one of those idiots at a nationalistic rally. Surely you are not that stupid."

"Look, are we not at war?"

"No, this is a special military operation. You just said so yourself."

"Then let me rephrase. Are our people sustaining injuries in this activity?"

"Too many."

"Do you not think it best to have as many medical specialists available to help?"

"I do."

"Then, for Christ's sake, let me in."

"Madam, I would, but you will not get far with the vehicle you are in. All the roads are damaged beyond repair. The only vehicles able to travel are military-grade."

"Then take me with you."

The officer hadn't expected the request. "Wait here," he said.

Nina watched the man return to a shack, then emerge a few minutes later, shaking his head. She panicked.

Nina backed her Largus, then slammed it into drive and gunned the engine. She scraped between a BTR-90 and a concrete pylon, only to end up in a clearing where she had to give up. Her Largus was surrounded by a collection of military vehicles hogging every inch of real estate.

"Now, Madam," the officer condescended once he caught up, "what the hell was that all about?"

"I panicked," Nina replied. "I am desperate to get to my post. You looked like you were about to tell me no."

"And looks can be deceiving," the officer replied. "Now, get out of the vehicle and follow me."

Nina managed to back the Largus free of the pylon. She had to lean into the damaged door to force it open.

"Madam, what you saw was a man frustrated by the moral logic of his superior officer. I made your case in the shack, expecting my commander to say no."

"And did he?"

"He did not. He said if you want to advance to the front and help our wounded, have at it."

"This is good news."

"No, it isn't. You will likely be killed."

"That's a chance I must take."

Nina looked back to see her vehicle amid the armament, knowing it would be nothing more than a bump under the tread of their advance.

"And forget about your car," the officer said. "You will have to ride with us, making things worse for you."

"Can I at least take my suitcase?"

"No, it is flammable and will get in the way of the soldiers in the vehicle. I suggest you wear battle-ready clothing. And remember, what you put on will be what you have on for quite some time."

Nina ignored the insult. "At least I'll have protection," she said with compensating encouragement.

"Not really! The Ukrainians are adept at taking our vehicles out, so you may find yourself on the receiving end of a Stugna-P missile."

"Again, it is a risk I must take."

"Then let me pose this one last reality to you. These vehi-

cles are not like a Largus riding on smooth pavement. You will
be jostled around and thrown against the interior walls. A
woman your age may find herself badly bruised by the time she
gets to her destination."

Again, Nina passed on the insult.

"And speaking of destinations," she pressed beyond the
warning, "I am to head toward Kiev?" Nina knew that by using
the Russian pronunciation for the city, she sounded more
convincing.

"We have not yet taken Kiev," the officer returned, "but
there is a column advancing to the north of the city."

"Then take me there. I'm sure I will be able to connect with
my comrades."

"So be it." The officer abruptly stopped to look Nina in the
eye. "Madam, you are a fool."

"And you are not a patriot."

The officer ignored the comment and directed her to a
bench outside the office.

"I will get my things first," she responded.

Nina returned to the Largus, opened the hatch and
unlatched her suitcase. She had packed a blue pair of
Gorbachev-era pants with enough pockets to carry more than
her keys and identification. This reminded her to pull the keys
out of her skirt pocket and toss them into the driver's seat.

"These are no longer useful."

Next, she selected a tan shirt, embroidered folk accessories
and a pair of socks heavy enough to keep her feet warm. Next
to the suitcase, she had packed her late husband's work boots,
partly because they reminded her of him but mostly because
they happened to fit her.

Nina grabbed the crucifix, shoved it into a pant pocket, and
then proceeded to the shack.

"Is there a place where I can change," she asked when she
opened the door.

"Lady, what are you doing in here? Get out."

"I need to change my clothes. I am about to leave with the next convoy."

"Oh, it's you, the so called nurse."

"This must be the commander," Nina thought.

"Okay, behind this office screen, and be quick about it."

Nina changed and then returned to the shack's porch.

"It feels good to be in fresh clothing. A shower would have been better."

She sat and stared at the amassed equipment. There was nothing except her Largus to remind Nina of her old world. Everything was the filth of armour, demoralized soldiers and an intended attack on humanity.

And what lay ahead? She tried not to think of it. Instead, she slept.

8

EXPLOSION

Hearing was the only sense alerting Wassil to what was happening. He could hear the shells creep closer to their position.

The bunker was dark, with only a few hand-held lights and cell phones rationing their remaining power to periodically illuminate small areas. There was one exception. A bright glow leaked from around a corner.

"That is where Mrs. Melnyk is giving birth to her third child," an inmate had informed him. "Can you believe it? She is giving birth in a filthy place that once was a popular sushi restaurant."

"What have we done?" Wassil thought.

Someone moving close to him turned on the light of their cell phone. It was Lidiya.

"How far would you say those explosions are happening?" He asked her.

"You sound like a spy," Lidiya replied.

Wassil chuckled. "I doubt people would think me capable of such an intricate profession."

"Intricate?"

"Yes. Doesn't a spy need refined networking skills and an agile mind?"

"And a deep sense of patriotism." Lidiya completed the list.

"Then I am no spy!"

"Not to worry. You didn't strike me as one."

"And isn't that exactly what a spy would want you to think?"

"Touché!" Lidiya smiled.

There was another whistle followed by an even louder explosion. This one loosed plaster and concrete from the bunker ceiling, showering those inside in pebble-sized debris.

"I suppose we will be moving west soon," Lidiya announced.

"To Rivne?"

"Perhaps."

"I was there once. Two years ago, on vacation with my mother."

"Your father did not come?"

Wassil took advantage of her question, even though he did not like to talk about losing his father. In this situation, the conversation might help distract from the chaos around.

"He was killed when I was twenty, apparently by a bomb in Syria."

"How sad."

"Yes, but I was glad to be there for my mother – until the army called when I turned 26."

Another cell phone lit up, and Wassil used the light to look at Lidiya. "Mother was not happy."

"I'm sure she wasn't," Lidiya reciprocated with a long stare into Wassil's blue eyes. "So you've been in the army for a year?"

"It was a job, plus I'm looked after. I also get 2200 roubles a month. I send most of it to my mother."

"That is not much money. Could you not make more with an army trade?"

"I suppose, but we are shipbuilders in Shlisselburg. It is the only trade I know. There's not much call for it in the army."

"Then your army is not very good with its Human Resources, eh?"

Wassil let out a short guffaw. "Lidiya, you are correct on that point."

"Attention, everyone," a voice called over a megaphone. "We are moving out. But please hear this; know the Russians have not agreed to a humanitarian corridor, so what we are about to do will be at your own risk. You can follow us and risk destruction in the open air by artillery shells, or you can stay here and risk the same destruction in a hole."

"Jesus," Wassil said to Lidiya. "Some choice."

"You think?"

"I wish I could stop this."

"Well, you can't! Please stand. I am told you will be going first."

"Why is that?"

"Don't know. Commander's orders."

"They probably want me as a shield."

"Oh, that's just great. That means me too."

"How so?"

"I am to accompany you."

Wassil couldn't see Lidiya but could feel her grab at his arm, not with the cruel aggression of a prison warden but with the care of a scout escorting an old person across a street.

He reached to put his hand on hers. Lidiya did not pull away.

"Get ready," she said.

"For what?"

"You'll see."

A moment later, the room lit up. Someone had restored the lighting system, and for the first time, Wassil could survey his entire environment. He saw people sitting motionless, a few talking, all freezing in the damp cold temperatures. Children hugged their parents while their parents cried. The older people sat alone, dejected. Everyone was filthy.

"We are to lead these people out of here."

"Then I will lead on. I am ready."

Wassil stepped over two prone people into a small clearing.

"This way," Lidiya directed to the entrance. "And watch your step."

"You seem to have more faith in me than what is warranted."

"I am only working on getting us out of here safe."

"Are you not afraid I might attack or try to escape."

"Not in the slightest! Besides, how much worse could you make it? I need to take a chance, and you seem like a safe bet."

Wassil did not get a chance to respond. At the entrance, he heard an ear-splitting whistle and then felt the shock of a blast. Concrete collapsed, dust rose, and Lidiya disappeared. Wassil was thrown against a fading mural of some great Ukrainian event.

"Lidiya!"

There was no answer.

"Lidiya!"

Again, nothing.

He began to feel around and eventually felt a boot, Lidiya's boot. It was shaking, probably from shock.

Wassil began to dig. He was glad to be out of his cuffs. Luckily, two pieces of concrete had fallen against each other, forming a crude triangle and preventing Lidiya from being crushed. He dug into the centre of the triangle, calling her name.

Wassil knew he had little time. Lidiya would already be close to suffocation.

When he got to her waist, he tried pulling her legs. It was a crude move, but he was afraid of the time she had already spent covered. His effort worked. He heard a cough, signalling life which renewed his motivation.

"Thank goodness," he yelled into the pile. "Lidiya, I'm here. Hang on."

Wassil furiously clawed at the debris, brushing aside rubble and blood.

"I'm here," Lidiya finally coughed. "I'll be fine. Check on the others."

Wassil did as she requested. Most of the damage happened at the entrance where another large slab of concrete prevented people from evacuating the building. Wassil signalled a man near him to help move the slab aside.

They had no luck, but that changed after more people showed up to force the slab away from the entrance.

Once done, people began to file out.

Wassil stayed with Lidiya.

9

CHERNIHIV

The sound seemed oddly out of place.

"Why would a warbler be singing in the middle of winter?"

Wassil played bandy on Shlisselburg's largest rink. Nina giggled at the sight of him deking the defence, scoring a goal, then kidding the players on both teams.

Then came the roar of a diesel motor, and Wassil faded with it into the background. There was no hint as to why and no trace of what had become of him.

"Uh, what time is it?"

"Pardon me, my little cutie," replied a young, green-eyed soldier, apparently amused to be questioned by a vagrant on the porch of the command office.

"What time is it?" Nina raised her voice.

"It's almost morning, and it's about to get noisy."

"What?"

"That's right, Madam, we're about to move out."

The green-eyed soldier winked, then scurried to a nearby troop carrier. He stopped at its rear, then veered to the left.

"I can't believe I slept," Nina said, watching the soldier being absorbed into the war machine. "I've lost valuable time."

She stood to take in the compound. Everything was different, and her vehicle was gone.

"Easy come. Easy go," she thought.

What did bother her was the array of equipment. All the military vehicles were either moved or replaced.

"How could I sleep through this much commotion?" She asked herself. "No matter, I need answers."

Nina walked into the commander's shack without knocking.

"Why was I not informed when you were moving out?" She demanded of the new duty officer. "I need to be included in the next group."

"Slow down, Madam. I was given strict instructions to let you sleep off whatever you had too much of. I'm just doing my job."

"Don't get smart with me. I demand to be included with the next convoy."

"Oh yes," he replied. "I was also told you had delusions of being a nurse and were destined to help our comrades on the front."

"And what makes you think I am delusional. I, like you, am Russian. We look after our own, do we not?"

"Yes, we do, but not with people like you. Madam, please return to your home."

Nina remembered the previous officer's return to the shack.

"I will not," she replied. "I have permission from your commanding officer. Let me speak with him."

"He's not here."

"Then get him. I must be on your next convoy."

"I will not."

"Then, I will report you as disobedient."

"Go ahead. Be my guest."

"I will."

"Madam, you do not have the nerve."

"Look, I've already put up with a lot of bullshit getting here. Do I look like someone who backs down from a challenge?"

"Fine. I'll make a call. You wait outside so I can speak with the commander in peace."

Nina returned to the porch to give the officer a chance to chat in private and, no doubt, to complain. She used her time to survey the surroundings, which proved difficult as plumes of black smoke built up with the starting of the vehicles.

"Hey."

Nina couldn't hear over the din of diesel motors.

"Hey!"

It was the officer calling at her from the doorway.

"See the last troop carrier," he yelled, "the one with the open hatch on the side?"

It was the same one the green-eyed soldier entered.

"Yes."

"There's a seat in it for you. You'd better make it fast."

The officer hadn't finished his sentence when Nina started running.

She fumbled for a foothold and finally found one on the side the carrier. She used it for leverage and, with a single push, lifted herself into the machine. The soldier closest to the door instinctively grabbed her arm to pull her in.

"What the hell," one of them said, "are we recruiting old women now?"

"Shut up," the carrier's commander yelled into the cab. "I'm not happy about it either, but I have my orders."

Nina found herself sprawled across the laps of two soldiers, and from that position, she raised her head to locate her seat.

"Hey, it's 'little cutie' come to visit. Welcome to the BTR-80! We'd put you in a 90, but that's for fancy soldiers only. Not conscripts."

Everyone laughed.

Nina was shoved to the right, deep into the carrier, farthest from an exit. Before she could right herself in her seat, the BTR-80 lurched ahead. Her head banged hard against the ceiling.

"God damn," she yelled.

"You're supposed to be wearing a helmet," the soldier nearest to her said before turning away to engage his comrades. A moment later, he passed an old helmet to her.

"Here, take this. You're going to need it when things get rough."

The helmet was too big for Nina, but it was better than nothing.

The next jolt was far more aggressive, and she found herself in the lap of her green-eyed soldier.

"We have to stop meeting like this," he said.

More laughter.

"Is this what I have to look forward to?" She asked.

"Ah, my little cutie, we are going to Chernihiv and not along the usual roads. What usually takes an hour and a half will take us three hours. So yes, it is going to be rough."

"Stop calling me 'little cutie.' I am not in the mood for it."

"Then what will you have me call you?"

"Nina."

"Then Nina it is. I am Fedor. I am named after our greatest writer."

"Good. Now, Fedor, when do you expect to be in the danger zone?"

"We're in it already. Madam, you are in Ukraine, on your way to Kyiv via Chernihiv."

"And does that bring me closer to Rivne?"

"Rivne? What is in Rivne?"

Nina realized she was on the cusp of giving up too much of her mission.

"Nothing, it's just that after Kyiv, we go through Rivne. It was a town I spent time visiting in years past. After that, I assume we're on to Lviv before reaching the Polish border and completing our special operation."

"Then you and I must learn not to assume too much. War is chaos."

Fedor leaned into Nina. "I should tell you that you are looking at a group of conscripts who do not care to be in Ukraine. Before this, we were as happy in our homes as the Ukrainians were in theirs."

"I see," Nina acknowledged.

A tear welled in his left eye. "We'll be lucky if we get out of this alive."

10

THE FIRST SHOTS

Two and a half hours had passed, and Nina resigned herself to the rough ride. Glimpses through the vehicle's portholes gave her a sense of the war-rugged terrain. The bruises on her arms, legs and back made that sense real.

"Standby," came a sharp order from the commander.

"Standby?" Nina shouted the question into Fedor's ear.

"It's a warning. It means we've picked up on enemy activity. I suspect the vehicles at the head of the column have already deployed. We are to make ourselves battle-ready."

"Enemy?" The word hit hard. "These people are not our enemy. They are our neighbours."

"Do you not think I already know that?"

"On my mark," the commander yelled into the vehicle.

Nina realized these men had been drilled on what was about to happen. She hadn't. A panic set in as she waited.

"Here we go, boys," the commander yelled again. "Out. Out. Out."

The BTR-80 slammed to a halt, and Nina fell forward into

Fedor. Somehow, the hatch opened, and the soldiers spilled into the Ukraine countryside.

"Wait a few minutes before leaving," Fedor instructed Nina as he uprighted her in her seat. "We will make sure it is safe."

He leapt out the hatch into a din of small arms fire. Nina could not see them from her position, but she heard the thud of bullets hitting the vehicle. Then it stopped.

"For Christ's sake," the commander yelled, "get us out of here. Now!"

Nina sensed a commotion up front as the driver tried to engage the vehicle as commanded. It did not move.

"Out. Out. Out. Now!" The commander screamed in desperation.

Nina pulled her bruised body from the seat and made for the side door. She saw the driver and commander scramble from their seats through the hatches above. They disappeared, but only for a moment. Both fell back into their seats, covered in blood.

"Oh God," Nina cried out before gripping the edge of the hatch and pulling herself from the vehicle.

Nina stepped down and tripped across the corpse of a soldier. It was Fedor. He had been shot so many times his face was barely recognizable.

"Oh God," she cried out again. "What is happening?"

From her prone position, Nina scanned the area. All the soldiers who had accompanied her lay dead.

"Run."

Nina heard the word and saw a small group of soldiers aiming a weapon in her direction.

"My poor Fedor." Nina uprighted herself, ignoring the threats around her. She knelt beside his body, looking for an unbloodied spot to lay a remorseful hand.

"Madam, out of the way. Please."

The please in the request alerted her to the safety in their direction.

Nina ran toward them as a missile approached, passing her dangerously close overhead. It slammed into the BTR-80.

❀

"Madam, are you all right?" Asked a nurse on her left in perfect Russian.

"I am."

"Here, try this." A woman on her right held a spoon to her mouth.

Nina turned her head away.

"Madam, you must eat something," she pleaded.

"Where am I, and who are you?"

"Welcome to Ukraine!" Came the voice from the foot of her cot.

"And you speak Russian?"

"We are Slavonic brothers and sisters. We prefer Ukrainian but can adapt for guests. Our languages are not that different."

"I see," Nina replied.

The woman pulled up a chart and began leafing through its pages.

"I only wish our meeting could have been more civil," she said without looking at her. "However, some people insist on seeing us as an enemy. But let us put that aside for the moment. I am Kathy, and this is Brenda on your left and Lori on your right. We will escort you to safety."

"Thank you. I am Nina, and I am looking for my son."

Nina lifted her head to scan the room. She saw the ruins of what once served as a medical clinic.

"Pardon me?" Kathy asked.

"My son. Wassil," Nina said with her eyes fixed on an opening that once held a window. "You captured him and are keeping him prisoner. I was told I could take him home if I came to get him. When can I see him?"

"Madam, you have sustained injuries and are likely confused from the blast's shock. You will need to rest for a few days."

"I am not confused, and I need to get to Rivne."

"I'm sorry. Rivne is on the other side of Kyiv, a two-day journey."

"Then I must start now."

"This will likely prove difficult."

"Why?"

"Because the land between here and Kyiv is a killing waste-land. You would need to get across that first then, if you made it, you would be competing with thousands of refugees moving west to the Polish border."

"Then, am I to take it we are staying here?"

"For the moment, yes."

"That is not acceptable."

"I didn't want to bring this up," Kathy moved from the foot of her bed to her right side. "But you are also a prisoner."

"How can that be? I'm not a soldier."

"But you came in a military vehicle."

"I was hitching a ride to get my son."

"And the Russians thought that would be a good idea?"

"I had to fight with them, but eventually, they said yes."

"Nina, that makes so sense."

"It does if you pretend to be a nurse."

"You were lying to them?"

"Yes. To get my way."

"Then, well played. But that does not change your current position. We still need to treat you like a prisoner."

"I do not care what you call me or how you treat me. Just bring me to my son."

11

THE WALK

Wassil had already moved Lidiya's legs to help her get air after the blast. He was afraid to move her again. "What if her back is broken," he asked himself. "I could make things worse."

"Wassil!" Lidiya's voice echoed feebly from under the concrete wedged above her.

"I am here."

"And everyone else?"

"All escaped, except us. It's just you and I."

Wassil crouched closer.

"Lidiya, are you able to move?"

She tried raising herself on her elbows but was prevented by a length of rebar close to her head.

"And if I place my arms under you, do you think I could try sliding you out?"

"I think so."

Wassil gently pushed his arms under her back and then tried lifting enough to reduce her drag on the ground. His first effort gained a centimetre.

"Owwww."

Wassil stopped.

"No, keep going," Lidiya urged. "I am fine."

Wassil tried again, this time moving her ten centimetres.

"Better," Lidiya responded. "Again."

Wassil repositioned himself and then put his all into the next attempt. He was able to clear the rebar and the concrete.

"Wonderful," Lidiya coughed, "thank you."

"You are most welcome, but can you move?"

Lidiya tried her elbows again. It took some effort, but she succeeded.

"And what about standing? Do you think you can do that?"

Lidiya tried moving her legs. Nothing. Her face distorted with the second exertion. Still nothing.

"Then let me help."

"No, no. I'll get it."

"But we need to get out of here now. I fear my countrymen will start bombarding this place again."

"Then perhaps you're right."

With that, Wassil lifted Lidiya and carried her to the hotel entrance. He had to steady himself to avoid bumping her against the jagged edges.

Once outside, he surveyed the landscape. Missile strikes marred every building. The roadways were littered with debris. He knew this wasn't going to be an easy walk.

"Which way is west?" he asked Lidiya.

"Behind you."

Wassil adjusted himself and Lidiya to his right and rounded the corner of the building, then proceeded up the roadway between the hotel and a row of apartment buildings.

Collapsed walls and ruptured city infrastructure presented him with a series of mounds and craters.

There was no way to get around the first crater. "Hold on," he said to Lidiya from the precipice. He plunged into its centre and used the momentum to help propel him up the other side.

Lidiya groaned.

"I'm so sorry," he blamed himself.

Fifty meters more presented a much more significant obstacle, this time a mound of rubble with random concrete and rebar barriers.

"I am so sorry to have to do this, but please hold on." Without the benefit of a railing or stair, he tramped his way to the top.

"You are good at this," Lidiya said. The awkward comment was all she was able to contribute to the effort.

"This will not be a day we will soon forget."

The top presented a new challenge – more concrete and rebar, only this time on the way down.

"Okay, Wassil," he muttered, "slow and steady."

Each step was deliberate and a fight against inertia. Wassil thought a conversation might help.

"Where did your people go?"

"I do not know," said Lidiya. "They are probably travelling the main road."

"That seems dangerous to me. I'm sure our heavy equipment will be using the road to advance. Your people will be exposed."

"Either way, they didn't waste time getting out."

"Such is the nature of war and of fear. Everything is done in a panic."

At the bottom, Wassil paused to take a breath. A half-hour passed.

"You must rest," Lidiya said. "You have been carrying me this entire time."

"I ... am fine," Wassil replied.

"But it is not right," Lidiya rebutted. "You must leave me. I'm sure someone will be along presently to take over."

"But I am your prisoner and unshackled. How would it look on your record if you let me escape?"

Lidiya stared at him, serious at first, before catching the pleading earnestness in his eyes. She let a smile cross her face.

"Wassil, you are a good man."

12

MORSELS OF CARE

"The people here are nice considering what they are going through," Nina spoke to no one in particular. She sat on one of two kitchen chairs set up for her in the corner of a medical tent. Staff encouraged her to rest on a cot, but she refused.

"It is bred in their character and professions," replied a tall woman dressed in a dark blue smock. Her hands flailed about restocking a medicine cart.

"Professions?"

"Yes, we are medical people like you."

"Like me?"

"Did I not hear that you are a nurse?" the woman asked.

"No, I am not. I only told the soldiers I was so they would let me pass into Ukraine."

"Ah. Clever. And what were you trying to accomplish coming to this tragic place?"

"As I told your officer, I am here to get my son."

"Your son?"

"His name is Wassil, and he was taken prisoner by your people. He is somewhere near Rivne."

"Oh my, that is on the other side of Kyiv."

"I tried crossing through Belarus, but they wouldn't let me. They directed me to a Russian border crossing instead."

The woman did not seem interested in Nina's logistics. "But the end is the same," she concluded, "we are both concerned with care, you as a mother for your son and I as a nurse for this humanity around me."

"But your care extends to so many people. People well beyond the confines of this tent."

"And yours to one," the nurse said emphatically. "Every morsel of care counts."

The nurse broke off the conversation to respond to an order.

Care became the lens from which Nina observed the activities in the tent. Ukrainian men and women were everywhere attending to wounded soldiers, most Ukraine, some guarded Russians. Too many suffered intense mutilations. Some were operable. Others were numbed and kept calm so they could die in peace. Civilians were being treated in the same areas. One Russian soldier rested on his elbows, his tear-filled eyes locked on an armless mother trying to comfort her child.

"Or is the child trying to comfort the mom?" Nina wondered.

Nina noted how the limited medical supplies were labelled with simple crosses and fancy brands, most from western sources. She was able to name a few and wondered how they managed to get to this particular tent.

The nurse returned, interrupting Nina's observations.

"And from there, you thought you could enter our country and pick him up?" She asked as if the conversation had not been interrupted.

"Pardon me?"

"From Russia, you thought you could drop into Ukraine and pick up your son?"

"I was told I could by one of your officers."

"I'm sure that was a rhetorical invitation," the nurse pointed out. "As you can see, this is a dangerous place. I'm sure the officer would not have been so insensitive as to invite you to this terror."

The nurse began to tear up as she finished the last sentence.

"Believe me, I had no idea we were inflicting this much harm," Nina responded.

"And I, too, had no idea we were so capable of resisting."

"And it must be hard."

The nurse took a seat in a chair next to Nina.

"I, like you, have a son somewhere in the battle. I worry about him every day and pray for his safe return."

"Return?"

"I know. My son's already here, just lost in his own homeland. There is no return other than victory or eventual death on the battlefield."

"And to what end?" Nina asked.

"Exactly."

Nina leaned over to comfort the nurse.

"I'll be fine. I just have to get back to work. It helps."

"And what is your name, my dear?" Nina asked.

"I am called Katrina."

"Hello Katrina, I am Nina."

"And Nina, I return to my question. What do you expect to happen?"

"I will press on to Rivne and look for my son."

"I cannot help you with that."

"I do not need your help unless you could provide me with a ride."

"I cannot do that either." The nurse stood to join her colleagues.

"I've noticed that many of your resources are foreign," Nina raised her hand to touch the nurse's arm. "I suspect they come from points west of here."

"They do."

"Then could I get a ride with your supply person the next time they head west?"

"That would be great, except that technically, you are a prisoner of war."

"I am not a soldier."

"But you arrived in a military vehicle."

"That is true. But in the interests of care, surely you can see the need to overlook this detail."

"In the interest of care, I can overlook any senseless military imperative. Unfortunately, it's not me you need to convince."

"Then who?"

"See the man standing by the desk at the entrance?"

"Yes."

"He is our commander."

13

DOCTOR KUZMA

Care is the key to everything. It manifested itself in Nina's love for her son, and it motivated her to cling to what was left of her family.

Nina hoped the commander would see it the same way she did.

"Excuse me."

"One moment, please," replied the commander with his pointer finger in the air.

"Be sure to prep *Soldat* Petruso first," he told a surgeon. "The Major can wait. Just have someone keep him stable."

The surgeon spun on his heels and disappeared into a throng of caregivers.

She hoped her encounter with the commander would be this fast and decisive in her favour.

"Now," the commander said, returning to Nina, "what can I do for you?"

"I would like a ride to Rivne." Nina thought it best to get to the point.

"Rivne? Madam, I am not a cab driver. You will need to bring that request to our motor pool."

"But I need your permission to leave."

"Are you a patient?"

"I was."

The commander took a step back to give Nina a scan, then returned to focus on her facial features.

"Oh yes," he said, "I recognize you. You are the Russian woman we captured in the BTR-80 attack. Madam, you can go nowhere. You are a prisoner."

"Then why am I not shackled?"

"That is a good question." The commander took another back step to look Nina up and down. "I do not see you as a belligerent. Perhaps others don't as well. They may feel there is no need for cuffs."

"No matter. I am not involved with this conflict."

"We are all involved with this conflict."

"But you don't understand. I am here to retrieve my son. He was captured and held somewhere near Rivne."

"Then you are definitively involved in this conflict."

"I see your point, commander." Nina did not want an argument. "But I was told I could retrieve him if I wanted. In fact, I was told so by someone of your rank."

The commander paused for a moment.

"Ah, yes, no doubt permission motivated by our President's invitation. I also heard the Russian mothers asking which door they should knock on to get their sons when they arrived. What I have not seen yet is a Russian mother take up the offer."

The commander accepted and signed a clipboard document from a nurse on the move. The action took him into a spin that he followed through on after releasing the clipboard into the nurse's hands.

"Madam," he said after landing the maneuver, "you are the first."

"So you will let me go?"

"I wish it was that easy. Have you been made aware of the dangers and obstacles?"

"I have."

"Then give me a moment to confer with my staff."

Nina returned to her chair. She caught the eye of the commander talking with Katrina. Both looked in her direction as if seeking confirmation on a judgment. When they broke off, Katrina returned to Nina.

"That was Dr. Kuzma," she announced.

"He is a busy man."

"We are all busy."

"And I noticed he too speaks perfect Russian?"

"We all speak Russian. We have to with so many wounded Russian soldiers in our midst. But you are missing the point."

"Sorry."

"Doctor Kuzma says you can go, but only if accompanied by one of our people."

"I do not mind."

"It's for your own good, you understand, not because he sees you as a military threat. From a military perspective, he doubts an unarmed person poses much of a threat to the security of Ukraine."

"Either way! It does not matter to me."

"Nina," Katrina took her hands, "I supported your request too, only because I need you to do me a favour."

"Anything I can, if possible," Nina responded, expecting a grave request.

"My son is in the thick of this battle, and I do not know where he is. I'm sure you can appreciate my concern. His name is Artem Bondar of Chernihiv. If you meet him or hear of him, will you tell him to contact me?"

"I will."

"But, there is more."

"Oh?"

"Will you contact me as well and tell me about him. You will appreciate what it is a mother needs to hear."

"I will."

Katrina quickly scrolled her cell number and email address on a paper for Nina.

"I do not know if either of these will get back to me, but promise you will try your best."

"I will," Nina replied.

Katrina watched her intently with the eyes of a desperate woman. Nina punched the number and address into her cell phone. Katrina smiled to see Nina carefully fold and place her note in her pocket as an added safeguard.

"Come here," Katrina said to Nina, drawing her in for a hug. "Thank you."

"You are welcome." Nina held Katrina at arms length and looked deep into her eyes. "I will try, but right now I must know how to get out of here?"

"I do not know."

"Dr. Kuzma mentioned a motor pool."

"I would not trust anything around here called a motor pool."

"And what about your supply people. Could I get a ride with someone returning for more medical supplies?"

"That would take another permission," Katrina replied.

"From who?"

"Dr. Kuzma."

"Then I will ask."

"No, let me," Katrina insisted. "Go outside and cross the road. You will see a parked van with a British pub logo on the side. It was donated by a merchant and has been readied to pick up a supply of surgical equipment and trauma packs. Be sure you get in the pub van. And yes, the driver speaks Russian too."

"Done," Nina replied, already on her way.

She presented at the van.

"Excuse me," she called through the open passenger window to the driver.

"Yes?"

"I was told I could get a ride with you on your next supply run."

"I have received no such order."

Nina lifted herself on her toes to better speak through the passenger window.

"Wait for it," she told the driver. "It should be along soon."

"It's okay. Kuzma has approved it," Katrina hollered from behind Nina.

"Fine. I could use the company anyway."

Katrina and Nina exchanged looks. Katrina winked, and Nina smiled. She knew Katrina did not have time to make the request.

14

THE DRONE

"And what is your name, my dear?" The driver asked while pencilling his departure time in a logbook.

"I am Nina."

"And how the hell did you end up in this place?"

"I am looking for my son."

"What is his name?" It occurred to Nina that the question had little chance of landing a suitable answer. She knew the driver would not know her son.

"He is called Wassil."

"A good Russian name."

"It is."

"You do know my primary job is not to escort or search for Russians?"

"I do, and please do not be upset," she answered. "He is a prisoner, and I am here to fetch him."

"Madam, you are crazy. Do you even know where he is located?"

"Somewhere near Rivne."

"Well, there's your first bit of luck because I am going to Lviv. Turns out I will be passing through Rivne."

"Then that is good luck indeed!"

"Our only problem will be crossing the Dnieper River. By all accounts, Russian shells and missiles have been systematically destroying the bridges."

"What will we do if we cannot find a bridge."

"We aren't even looking for one. I hate being disappointed. Besides, it would be suicidal."

"Then what?"

"We have a friend with a pontoon boat. There is a narrows north of Kyiv where many trees overhang the banks. We will take cover there, and when the time is right, he will take us across."

"Oh," Nina replied. "How shrewd."

"Shrewd? I call it survival."

Fifteen minutes passed.

"Do you like Irish music?" The driver asked out of the blue.

"I don't think I've ever heard it."

"Then buckle up, lady. We are going to jig our way to Rivne."

The driver pushed a CD into the van's player, and the music blasted. The volume was already on his favourite ear-splitting setting.

"Why do young people feel it important to destroy their hearing?" Nina asked herself.

The music played for an hour while they drove along the back roads of Mizhrichynskyi Park. Then the driver abruptly shut it off.

"Is something wrong?"

"We are getting close to Kyiv and the Dnieper. I must pull over to check for Russian activity."

The driver stopped under a tree and then climbed into the back. Nina heard him flip a switch before speaking unintelligible words. She looked and noted the driver wearing headphones.

"I wonder if they speak the same gibberish on the other end of the transmission?"

The tone of the gibberish rose and fell as bits of information were exchanged. None of it brought a smile to the driver's face.

"This could get dangerous," he said while returning to the front of the van.

"How so?"

"Apparently, the Russians have done their jobs. They've taken out all the bridges except for the ones they control. Their ground troops are now searching the banks to ensure there is nothing else to stop them."

"And this means?"

"My little hiding place may not be there."

"Then, what do we do?"

"Well, we avoid the risk," the driver said emphatically while stepping out and walking around the van. His hands rotated from head-scratching to jaw rubbing.

"He is a man deep in thought." Nina tracked the driver as he rounded the van. She decided against joining him to query further.

After three revolutions the driver returned.

"We travel south," he announced, "past Kyiv to another narrows near Kaniv. We have another boatsman there with a craft to take us across the river."

"This is good," Nina said.

"Except that it will add time to our trip. Twice."

"Twice?"

"Yes, south to Kaniv, north to Rivne."

"Damn," Nina cursed. "But, if it must be done, then so be it."

The driver did not look like he appreciated the comment. Nina could sense she was a pain to him.

❈

Violent tossing woke Nina from a deep sleep.

"It's good you have your seatbelt on," the driver said to her while his eyes oscillated from the road to a small dash screen and back.

"It would appear," Nina acknowledged through the jostling. "I must have fallen asleep."

"And it's good that you are awake."

"Not that I had a choice."

"Hang on. Things are about to get rough."

No sooner had the driver said the words when he violently swerved the van to his left. A second later, the earth exploded behind them. The force was enough to lift the back of the van but not sufficient to topple it completely.

The driver recovered control.

"Jesus, that was close," he said.

"What now?"

"Lady, you are full of questions. All I can say is hang on."

This time he veered to the right. Another explosion happened with the same result.

"You bastards don't have us yet," he said.

"How do you know when to do that?"

"I have a vehicle drone detection system," the driver said, nodding at his screen. "Pretty cool, eh?"

"You are full of surprises."

"Well, don't get too cocky. We have a way to go before getting rid of the damn thing."

"How do we do that?"

"We call our situation in. I mean, you call it in."

"Pardon me?"

"I need you to get back there and call for backup," the driver pointed his thumb behind a partition to the van's cargo area. "Our people will figure something out."

"I don't know how to do that," Nina screamed.

"I'll talk you through it."

"What if I can't."

"It's not like defusing a bomb in some crap-ass Hollywood movie. Just get back there and do as I instruct."

Nina lifted herself from the seat just as the driver swerved the van in another avoidance maneuver.

Nina slammed her head against the partition. "Good thing it is padded," she thought. "And where the hell is my helmet?"

"Sorry about that, but remember this. Always expect the unexpected."

"Okay. What do I do?"

"See those headphones?"

"Yes."

"Put them on, then flip the red switch on the transmitter."

"Transmitter?"

"Jesus woman, the big black box on the shelf."

"Got it."

"Now, say the following. 'Looking for arms support.'"

Nina spoke the words into the microphone.

"Okay, good. Our people have been tracking our GPS for some time, so you need to verify us."

"Verify us?"

"Lady, you need to confirm with them that it is us."

"Okay."

"Now, repeat the following numbers. '58552291' Got that?"

"58552291"

"Great, now tell them that."

Nina recited the numbers into the microphone.

"That's it?"

"Yup. Good job. Now get back up here and buckle in."

When he heard Nina's belt buckle click, the driver executed another evasive turn, overcompensating, putting the van into a tailspin. When the van stopped, he and Nina were staring directly at the pursuing drone.

"Cooooome on," the driver emphasized the words, hoping the airstrike would happen before the drone fired.

Nina froze.

Smoke emerged from the drone, but it wasn't the contrail of a missile. Instead, the air around it erupted, splaying shards of shrapnel, destroying the drone. The van was close enough to take several pieces through the windshield. One barely missed Nina's head.

Nina's driver was not so lucky. He had been saved and killed by his own people.

15

THE DNIEPER

"Nina, you need to move."

She sat motionless, staring at nothing, pounding the words repeatedly in her mind. Meanwhile, the dead driver sat slumped in his seat, bleeding the remnants of his life onto the floor.

"I've lost Fedor, and now I've lost you, my friend," Nina said, breaking her mantra. "And I didn't even ask you your name. Could I not have afforded you this one morsel of care?"

Nina gently placed her hand on the driver's arm.

"And I promise I will tell your story to my son when I see him next."

A static noise reignited an awareness beyond the van's cab.

"I am alone," Nina said while surveying the surroundings outside the van. The drone lay in ruins with a field of debris presented across the front of the shattered window. To her side, a dense cluster of trees and a highway told her this would be her way out. She couldn't remember if she was looking in the direction they came from or were going in.

The sound of static distracted her again.

"Where is that noise coming from?"

Nina heard it behind her and followed it to its source – the transmitter's headphones.

She put them on and noted how the transmitter was still operating from when she used it.

Nina reached for the mic.

"*Privyet!*"

"*Pryvit,*" came the reply. "Are you all right?" The speaker switched to Russian.

"I am fine. The driver is dead. I do not know what to do."

"Madam, did the driver give you instructions?"

Nina had to think.

"He mentioned a narrows we were to cross. I believe it was at..."

"Please do not mention the name over the radio," the voice interrupted. "You may be monitored."

"Then what do you expect me to do?"

"Follow through on the original plan. Can you do that?"

"I can try, but I'll have to remove my driver from the seat. What do I do with him?"

"Lay him on the floor of your vehicle and cover him with a sheet, if you can find one. If you can't, use a jacket."

"Okay. I will do my best."

"That is good. Then once you are done, please continue on your route."

"That would be nice, except I do not know where I am going."

"Do you see a GPS by the driver's seat? On the dashboard?"

"Let me look."

Nina returned to the front and looked over her driver's bloodied shoulder. The VDD was still on though she could not make much of what it was trying to communicate. Like her vehicle, it had the same model of GPS built-in.

"There is one," she reported.

"Do you know how to use it?"

"I do."

"Then punch in the name of the town and follow the route. Try taking detours from time to time, so you are less conspicuous on the main roads."

"Less conspicuous?" The absurdity of the word overwhelmed her, launching Nina into a rant. "This bloody-damn vehicle has a British pub logo emblazoned on the side. Except for the odd hamlet and stand of trees here and there, I stick out in the middle of a wide-open prairie. Plus, I'm travelling with a dead body. What the hell is wrong with you? It doesn't get more conspicuous than that."

"I can understand how you feel," came an acknowledging response, "but we can do nothing about that for the moment. Your safest bet is to proceed as planned and be careful."

The speaker's tone settled Nina. She sat in silence, collecting her thoughts before responding. "Okay, if you say so."

"Madam, we know this can be hard, and all we can do is try. We wish you the best."

Nina replaced the mic and headphones, exited at the back of the van, then opened the driver-side door.

"Well, my friend, it is my turn to drive."

Nina placed her hands on her driver's left shoulder and pulled him to the ground.

"Hey, you. Stop!" The words broke the silence outside the van.

Taking a body with her would not be an option. The voices were accompanied by the thuds of footsteps running in her direction. In a panic, Nina scrambled into the driver's seat.

"Jesus, so much blood," she wailed.

She started the van and slammed it into gear.

"I will ignore the blood..."

Shots rang out.

"... and the bullets."

16

THE SALON

There comes a time when the lightest loads are too heavy to carry.

Wassil set Lidiya down on a display sofa in the showroom of what once was a women's fashion salon. "From this angle, you will be able to view the shelled building of the city's main square, not that it's a treat in any way."

"You must be exhausted," she said to Wassil, ignoring the ruins.

"I'm fine. It might be good for us to rest here for a moment before pressing on. I'm not sure where I am, but at least we are going in the right direction."

"You are west of Kyiv in the small city of Zhytomyr."

"This is where I have been all this time? Not Rivne?"

"That is correct."

"And how far is Rivne?"

"About 200 kilometres."

"That is far," Wassil said, standing straight, his hand to his forehead. "We need transportation."

"You could use the time to look around," Lidiya suggested. "Perhaps there's a vehicle we can use."

"And leave you here? I don't think so."

"I will be fine."

"What if the shelling starts again?"

"Then it happens," Lidiya said. "We have no more control over the guns than the weather."

Wassil looked for a blanket as she spoke.

"And, I've one request," Lidiya continued.

"Anything," Wassil replied as he fished a crochet blanket from a supply closet.

"Could you move me away from this window? I feel exposed."

"Of course."

Wassil cleared another sofa in the room and moved it away from the window, closer to the exit."

"How is that?"

"Good. Thank you. I will be safe here."

"And I will keep you safe, I promise."

Wassil sat beside Lidiya, overwhelmed by the moment and leaned in to kiss her cheek. Lidiya raised her hand to reroute his lips. Their kiss was long and passionate, fusing every molecule of affection between them. In that touching moment, the war and their nation-states gave way to allow them to belong to each other. Everything was reset to a natural order of things.

When the kiss ended, Wassil tried speaking. All he managed was a stammer.

"Now go," she ordered with a smile. "See if you can find an abandoned vehicle for us."

"Okay, but not too far or too long. I will be right back."

Wassil's euphoria was abruptly erased when he returned to the street. The urgency of his mission muscled in as he scanned a square littered with the husks of cars and trucks.

The perimeter vehicles had been hit and gutted by fires.

Other vehicles in the middle of the square looked promising, except they were hemmed in by massive debris piles.

"Whoever orchestrated this attack knew what they were doing," Wassil thought. "Too bad, because if the better vehicles had been on the perimeter, it might have been easy to drive out."

There were a few promising trucks, but they turned out to be unusable.

"Wassil, you fool, you've gone too far. What do you expect to find here? You must take Lidiya to the outskirts and find a vehicle there."

Wassil felt he had already spent too much time away from Lidiya and decided to take his search back to the salon. He chose a challenging route that required him to climb the remains of a truck.

"The view from up here might help," he rationalized.

And it did. From the top, Wassil noticed something different. He spotted a motorcycle on its side fifty meters from the Salon entrance. Its tires had slid under a burned-out vehicle. The bike looked to be intact.

"Perfect," he gave a shout. "We can get out with this machine if it starts and as long as Lidiya can get on."

Closer to the bike, Wassil discovered the person he suspected was the bike's owner. Half of his blood-drenched body had been blown away.

"You never knew what hit you, my poor fellow. But know this. I will put your bike to good use. I promise."

Wassil pulled the bike from under the car.

"Well, that was easy enough."

He stood the bike before him to give it a quick inspection.

"Looks good!"

He straddled the seat and twisted the key. The engine sputtered but didn't start.

He tried again.

"Bam!"

The engine backfired. Wassil took a look around to see if he had attracted attention. All appeared quiet.

"Good," he said. "Now be a good bike and start for me, please."

The third time the bike came to life with a roar before idling to a purr.

"Perfect," he rejoiced, "we are good to go."

Except.

"Where do you think you are going with that?" A single Ukrainian voice came at him from behind. He could feel the person standing too close to allow him to pull the bike into the clear.

Wassil froze.

"Where the hell did they come from?" He asked himself.

"Did you not hear him, soldier?" A small group goaded him in unison from further back. Wassil could tell they were made up mostly of men, but he thought he heard the distinct pitches of women as well.

"Rivne!" It was the only thing he could think to say.

"Well, listen to that, my dear comrades," the man said. "He happens to be going to the same place as us."

Wassil tried playing dumb.

"Then we can travel together."

The group laughed.

"Now get off and turn around," their man demanded. "Slowly."

Wassil dismounted and, with his right hand, set the bike on its side as he had found it. The action took too long.

"Now turn," the man ordered. "Now!"

Wassil did as he was told.

"You do not look familiar," the man looked him up and down through the slit in his balaclava. He stood in front of the others, hood and clothing completely black. The others were dressed in brown battle fatigues.

"Where are you from?" The man continued.

"Kyiv," Wassil replied.

"And why are you here?"

"My girlfriend and I were escaping to the west."

It was the only thing he could think to say, but his answer made him realize what he must do to protect Lidiya.

"Your girlfriend? And where is she?"

"She was killed."

"Oh, too bad," an incredulous response followed by a loud bang.

It came from the salon.

"Hey," Lidiya yelled from the floor of the salon doorway. She had pushed the door open with enough vigour to slam it into an adjacent brick wall.

The ruckus startled the soldiers. They responded by spraying bullets in her direction. Lidiya figured this would happen and had already rolled behind the doorway.

"Stop!" Wassil yelled. "Stop!"

The leader saw no threat and gave the order. All went quiet, and Lidiya took advantage.

"Leave him alone, or I will have you reported," she yelled from behind the wall.

"Show yourself," the man ordered.

"Would you like me to get her, Major?" One of his soldiers asked.

In the meantime, Lidiya rolled back into view.

"And who are you to issue such an order from the floor?" The Major asked.

"I am called Lidiya Kuzma, daughter of Doctor Kuzma of the Kyiv field hospital. This man is called Wassil, and he is my prisoner."

Lidiya knew the last words in her answer were a mistake, but she was on a roll.

"Prisoner, eh? He tells me you are his girlfriend."

"He is my prisoner, and he has just escaped. I am taking him to Rivne."

"Then perhaps we could help you," one of the female soldiers volunteered. "Since he will be so much trouble to escort, we will happily have him executed for you."

"Do not be savages," Lidiya yelled. "He is a human and deserves dignity."

"He is Russian. Russians are not human."

"And is this the way we taught you to think?" Lidiya scolded. "Shame on you and your family."

"I do not think you are in a position to shame anyone, young lady," the Major responded. "From where I stand, you are aiding this man in his escape. I do not see any restraints on him."

"He does not need them. He like me – like us – is seeking safety from this cursed war."

"Do not include us in your list of cowards."

"Then do what you must. Just leave us alone. I can take it from here."

"Do not trifle me with absurdities," the Major scolded. You can take nothing from here."

"Or maybe the Russian is right," a male soldier suggested. "Perhaps she is his girlfriend. Perhaps they are both Russian."

"Do not be ridiculous," Lidiya replied. "Can you not hear the language I speak?"

"Good point, comrade," the Major acknowledged the soldier. "Take them and bind them while I figure out what to do."

17

DETOUR

It is not hard to ignore a pool of blood when you are being fired on.

Nina had sped far enough to take her out of firing range, or so she hoped. She slowed to check the compass in the rearview mirror and study the GPS. Both told her she was heading north.

"*Chyort!*" She cursed. "I will have to take the risk my driver avoided and cross at the north side of Kyiv."

The only trouble was she didn't know where the narrows were located. "I will have to play it by ear," she said aloud.

Nina noticed a troop carrier behind her in the distance. It was like the BTR-80 she travelled in, except without a gun turret on the top.

"Okay, let's do this," her foot tramping on the gas pedal. The troop carrier fell off into the distance, and after fifteen minutes, Nina found herself alone on the road.

"I guess there isn't much of a top speed on those things," she sighed.

The solitude allowed her to reflect on her son. Her eyes welled, remembering the abrupt ending of their last call.

"Please let that cut-off be a simple technical problem."

To avoid thinking the worst, she directed her attention to her environment.

"It is little wonder the country is referred to as a bread basket." She knew it was too early in the season to see crops maturing, but she could imagine the wholesomeness of ripened wheat fields.

Nina then remembered her driver's insistence on taking backroads. She knew she would not be able to retrace the ones he took.

"What would be the point," she thought. "Everything is empty and flat. It's not like we can hide in a forest."

Nina settled the van onto the H08 motorway, past places like Kavkaz, Yerkivtsi and Rohoziv.

"Of course," she spoke to the memory of her old driver as she passed through Rohoziv. "You took the backroads to avoid the eyes and guns in these smaller urban centres."

Nina now thought this was a good tactic.

"Except, where are the Russians?"

At Boryspil, the signs redirected her to Kyiv's Slavutych bridge. It was intact, and she expected to be stopped at a Russian checkpoint. She would carry on with her nurse's story.

"We'll keep our fingers crossed," she said as if her driver was alive and with her.

The closer she got, the more she realized the checkpoint was occupied by a dispersed group of Ukrainian soldiers.

"They must have retaken the city'" she thought.

Nina was flagged down before a group of soldiers cooking food over a bed of coals. She noted how they had fashioned a BBQ from the fin section of a dismantled missile.

"Humph," she sniggered, "the tail section of all missiles should be converted to BBQs."

"Purpose for your travel?" came an unenthusiastic question

from a soldier miffed at having been taken away from his cooking.

Nina strained for the Ukrainian words she needed.

"Hospital," Nina remembered. It was enough.

"Pull over at station A," he pointed with a skewer.

Nina pulled over and waited for an inspector to show. She hoped they would not look into the van, or if so, not in the front seat.

"So, you are returning to where for your supplies?" A woman approached the van from the blindside. Nina wasn't exactly sure what she was asking but took a chance.

"Rivne," Nina answered.

"Rivne?" The inspector looked over her clipboard, lifting one of the pages for something to be revealed. "I thought they were being picked up in Lviv?"

"Rivne," Nina said again.

"Ah, hence the pub van?"

"Yes," Nina took what she hoped would be the last one-word answer.

"Proceed." The inspector waved her hands down the street.

Once on the highway, Nina began to relax.

"See!" Nina said into the van's cab. "It only stands to reason that a fast-thinking woman in a British van would be a shoo-in at a checkpoint. This is wonderful!"

Nina scanned her GPS. The E40 would take her straight to Rivne.

"Wassil, I am on my way," she confidently declared.

Instead, the E40 was blocked by a second checkpoint.

"Where to?" The soldier asked with the same lack of enthusiasm as the first.

"Rivne."

"Sorry, Madam, the Russians left this road a mess when they retreated. It is closed. You will have to take the E373 through Bucha."

18

CLOSING THE STORE

Wassil was returned to the salon with his wrists zip-tied behind his back. He was pushed to the floor in front of the display sofa. Lidiya's hands were zip-tied too. The soldiers dragged her into the showroom and dumped her next to Wassil.

"I am sorry," Wassil said to her, "I should have been more vigilant."

"It is not your fault," Lidiya squirmed on the floor to get a better look at Wassil. "But I think you should know something. This man has lied to us about the Russians being less than human."

"I don't understand."

"Did you not see the white Z on his lapel?"

"I did not. What does it mean?"

"There are various meanings, but all signify one thing – support for Russia. My dear Wassil, these people may be Ukrainians, but they are also my enemy."

"Then they are my enemy too."

"Except they will likely treat you better than I."

"You expect them to harm you?"

"Likely."

"Then we must escape."

"Wassil. You don't have to. I will understand."

"Then understand this. Russian or Ukrainian, I will not let these people harm you."

"I appreciate your help, but you will likely come to harm."

"I do not care. Lidiya, you and I complete each other." The words rolled off Wassil's tongue with conviction and passion.

Lidiya's eyes watered. "Then let us focus on an escape plan," she said.

Wassil could not tell if her words were said to process his admission of devotion or buy time to calculate a plan. But when he looked into her eyes, he saw longing, a future, a yearning to be with him. Even though she had not echoed his words, Wassil felt this was her expression of love.

"First," Wassil shook himself out of the moment, "we must get out of these ties. I've seen a lot of internet videos on how to escape them."

"I have watched a few too," Lidiya said.

"Then I will look for an opportunity to slide up onto the sofa, stand and slam my arms into my ass to snap the ties."

"I've seen that method."

"While I do that, you roll onto your side, flat on the floor. Let me overtake whichever guard is paying the least attention and use him to get to the other."

"It is a bad plan, my Wassil."

It was the first time he heard Lidiya speak possessively of him. His beaming pride was distracted by the Major's return. He went straight to Lidiya and grabbed her by the armpits to lift her to the sofa.

"Don't hurt her," Wassil demanded, "or I swear I will kill you."

"Oh, relax, Russian. I only want to talk to her."

The Major cupped Lidiya's chin in his hand to ensure her full attention.

"My people confirm that you are the daughter of the good doctor. But help me. I do not understand how or why this man came to be your prisoner."

"Yes. I am the doctor's daughter. What of it?" Lidiya tried shaking the man's hand from her face.

"Well, listen to you?" The Major jeered. "A minute ago, you announced it as if it were a big deal. Now it's nothing?"

"I only wanted to get your attention before you harmed this Russian."

"Oh, don't worry about him. What I want to know is where did you intend to take him?"

"To Rivne."

"Well, at least that's consistent with what he says." The Major gave a matter-of-fact nod to Wassil.

"We originally captured him in Kyiv," Lidiya continued. "We held him in a bunker until a missile struck."

"And now you are here. In Zhytomyr. Am I to believe his comrades are in and around these parts?"

"I do not know."

"Well, I think you do."

"And you," the Major abruptly released Lidiya's chin. "What were you doing in Kyiv?"

"Isn't it obvious?"

The Major slapped Wassil hard, knocking him onto his side.

"Very funny. What were your objectives?"

"That, Sir, is a good question. My unit was still on maneuvers in Belarus. I was surprised to find my unit advancing into Ukraine defending against counterattacks."

"And this unit? Where is it?"

"I don't know. I became separated from my comrades. They can be anywhere if they are not dead."

"Let's hope they are not," the Major concluded.

"Here is what we are going to do. Your girlfriend is officially a hostage. We will contact her father and make our one demand known. We want to know where our soldiers are being held."

"Then you will let Wassil go."

"No. While we may admire your boyfriend's comrades, I am unsure of his commitment to his motherland. He will remain with you."

19

BUCHA

"If I can get past those two checkpoints, getting through Kyiv to Bucha shouldn't be a problem. Even in this absurd van."

Nina had never been to a war-torn city before. Under normal circumstances, she would look for landmarks to reassure her – a famous coffee shop, a trendy clothing outlet, a favourite sports facility. These cultural beacons sat unrecognizable in this part of Kyiv. The streets were littered with vehicles and rubble, though paths had been plowed to allow traffic to pass. Moving was slow. Every few minutes, she checked her GPS to make sure she was on course.

There was some relief at the E373. Nina drove west and through the Holosiiv National Park with few obstacles. An hour later, she passed the gentle Horvenka marshes. Bucha was next.

Bucha was a town like any other. Its slight significance for Nina was that it held the road that would take her to her son.

A road sign announced Bucha as a railway town. She expected the traffic to move slower and was able to enter along Shevchenka Street. She drove past the Ukrainian Institute of Arts and Science before being stopped.

"The 373 is closed ahead. You will have to travel south," a checkpoint soldier said, pointing up a secondary roadway.

"Rivne," Nina said again. She was getting good mileage out of the name.

"No matter, lady. Figure it out."

"Thank you."

"And one more thing." The soldier halted himself in his turn around. "Be warned. This last attack has been particularly devastating."

Nina had no idea what the soldier was talking about.

She pulled away from the soldier and turned left. From there, driving was nothing but confusion. Nina eventually found herself in the hell of Yablunska Street.

The debris along the road was the same as the other streets except for a corpse lying alone behind a delivery truck. Nina noticed how the Ukraine soldiers patrolled the street, scarcely paying attention to the body.

"They have security priorities," she reasoned.

Nina guided her van to avoid the truck and body. She hoped to find a spot to turn around.

"Too many soldiers," she told herself.

She was not prepared for what lay ahead.

"Oh, Sweet Jesus," she cried out.

A patchwork of dead bodies slapped her hard. Women, men, and children dressed in the colours of daily life lay in pools of blood. All had been felled by bullets, some with their arms tied behind their backs. They had been executed. Blood was everywhere.

Nina heaved in the fight to cry and to be sick simultaneously. She tried looking away, only to find herself staring down a laneway strewn with more bodies, alone, mutilated. It was enough to break the tie. Her sickness mixed with the drying blood of her driver to produce an overwhelming moment of horror, sadness, and disgust.

Nina's hands froze on the wheel. She pulled back to free herself, then fumbled through tears for the door latch. Once outside, she tripped over a nearby corpse. It was a little girl face down in her own blood. She instinctively crouched to rub her back in an attempt to free her from whatever anxieties may be accompanying her journey to the next life.

"My child. What have I done to you?"

Nina's remorse was so deep she did not feel the hand on her shoulder.

"Go in peace, my child and forgive me."

"Madam," a voice said, "are you all right?"

Nina started rocking back and forth.

"Madam."

"Soldier, do you know what this is?" She responded in Russian.

"Madam, please," he replied, not noticing her language. "Perhaps it would be best to seek shelter."

"This is the product of my country's human resources set upon this child, this little person." Nina sobbed, raising her arm to take in the bodies around her. "All these persons."

"Madam. Are you saying you are Russian?"

"I am, and at the moment, not a proud one."

"Then it is doubly unsafe for you to be here. The people here are traumatized, aggrieved, and will seek revenge."

"Then let them have me. Hate begets hate. In this case, let these people express their rage. I will not oppose them."

The soldier stood dumbfounded, not knowing what to do. He tried a different tact.

"Madam, if you are Russian, what are you doing here?"

The question startled Nina. She had to force herself to consider an answer.

"Oh dear God. Wassil," Nina yelled into the sky. "Tell me you were not a part of this!"

"Excuse me?" The soldier asked. "Please, madam. You need to rest. Allow me to escort you away from this."

"My son." Nina ignored the offer. "I have come for my son, Wassil. He was taken prisoner somewhere near Rivne."

"You have come for your son. That's absurd."

"The prison commander said I could. Your president said I could. And so I did."

"Still. Did you really think you could succeed?"

Who was this soldier pestering her in a time of existential grief? Who was he to interrupt a wailing woman? Who the hell was he to be looking at this situation without being on a side?

"I did, and I need you to help."

"Excuse me?"

"I need you to arrest me, to take me to your prison."

"Why would I do that?"

"So I can be with my son."

20

ARREST

"Madam. I can arrest you, but I doubt it will help you find your son. Besides, everything in place for Russian prisoners is improvised and certainly undisclosed."

"But I was told my Wassil was being held somewhere near Rivne. I am to surrender myself. Apparently, that will help get me to him. It's the only chance I have."

The soldier considered.

"Okay, I will see what I can do, but you must follow my orders, understand?"

"I will do my best."

The soldier called out to a nearby officer. "Captain!"

"Yes," the Captain called back.

"Excuse me, Madam. I will be right back."

❋

"Captain, we have an issue. We need to arrest that woman over there."

"On what charge?"

"Charge? There is no charge. She's a Russian."

"Better to kill her then," the Captain replied.

"No."

"Why not? She's a Russian," the officer's flippant tone indicated how the conclusion should have been obvious.

"She's a person."

"But she's still a Russian."

"Yet, still a person."

"Look around you, son." The Captain changed his approach. "Her people did this, and she should pay for their losses, their sorrows."

"Don't be an animal, Captain." The soldier overstepped his authority. "She is a mother who was told by our people to surrender herself so she could find her son. Her nationality does not matter. It is an abstraction at best. She will always be a person."

"What the hell does that mean?"

"Captain, if you need to see this in 'us versus them' terms, that's one thing. But before we start expressing our anger, consider that this woman is making the supreme sacrifice. She is not only trying to rescue her son, but she is doing it in protest against her own government."

"How the hell is she doing that?"

"By plucking her son, this woman is saying no to war."

"And if she is successful, you know the Russians will shoot her for treason. They'll also execute her son for cowardice if and when they get home?"

"And that is different from being shot here?"

"At least if her son dies here, the Russian propaganda machine will hold him up as a hero."

"Here? No. Like most soldiers, he'll be consumed and forgotten. That is it."

The soldier repositioned his stance to face an awaiting Nina. "All I know," he said, "is we have a chance to show the world our capacity for compassion, which is the last thing dictators want their people to think."

"I still don't get you."

"Sir, it's easy to be angry. Any idiot can do it, and it makes everyone sad. On the other hand, it can be hard as hell to be peaceful. So, here's the point."

The soldier returned his gaze to the Captain.

"Power has duped people into fighting a war this woman and her son do not want to engage in. This is their chance to say no – to choose peace."

"Soldier, I don't need the lecture, but I concede this. You are brave and caring!"

"I don't know about that, Sir, but I am certain this woman is a hero."

"Then take her to Rivne."

21

TWENTY MINUTES

The Major returned with news.

"Well, guess what? We contacted your father, and he said to say hi. Nice man."

"He will tell you nothing," Lidiya scowled to discount the Major's cruel sincerity.

"And so far, you are correct. Your father hasn't said anything because he's busy begging for your life."

"Bastard!" Lidiya spat back.

"Come, come. This is a good thing. I'm giving your dad time to calm himself and think of his actions' consequences."

"Then what?" Wassil asked.

"Then it's demand time," the Major snapped. He pulled a chair to sit in front of Lidiya.

"Lady Lidiya," the Major said, his sarcasm so close to her face she spat. "Our demand is simple" He used his index finger to wipe the spit without moving his face. "Your father will tell us where we can liberate our comrades."

"You leave him alone," Lidiya yelled. "He has work to do. Some of it is to help your so-called comrades. Will you put them in danger?"

"We are already working on a plan for their liberation. But I will not concern myself with that at the moment."

The Major pushed his chair back to include Lidiya and Wassil in his view. He leaned his elbows on his knees and sat clasping his hands.

"What do you think? A pretty simple request, eh?"

"He will not know that information," Lidiya insisted, "and he would not tell you even if he did."

"Then I guess it will be up to you to persuade him."

"I will not."

"And if your father does not, your boyfriend dies." The Major flipped his thumb toward Wassil. "And that's just for starts."

"But Wassil is Russian. You wouldn't kill a comrade, would you?"

"Oh, please don't start pleading for his life too. I don't give a shit. Just know this. If Wassil dies, it will be your fault and your father's fault."

"You are a cruel bastard," Wassil raged. "If I get the chance, you will pay!"

"Oooooh, big words for someone so little at the moment," the Major responded. "I will be back in an hour."

❋

"What will I do?" Lidiya asked as the door closed behind the Major.

"What will we do?"

"My dearest Wassil, I do not want you involved in this any longer. You must look after yourself. You must go home to your family. You must be safe."

"Lidiya, I am home."

"You are far from home."

"I am with you."

"But you have a mother."

"And she is safe in Shlisselburg. I will deal with her situation when the opportunity arrives. Right now, we need to get out of here."

Tears streamed down Lidiya's cheeks. "I think these soldiers will have something to say about that."

"What about our original plan?"

"It is foolish," Lidiya replied.

It was also moot.

The Major returned early.

"I regret to inform you, but it looks like I am needed elsewhere, so we will deal now."

An adjunct handed the Major a cellphone. Dr. Kuzma's number had already been dialled.

"Dr. Kuzma?" He waited a moment for a response.

"Oh, good. And I hope you are doing well." The Major eyed Lidiya as he absorbed profanity in his earpiece. After a few minutes of bitter and abusive language, he decided enough was enough. "I need you to listen to me carefully. We have your daughter and her boyfriend and are prepared to let them go in exchange for a small piece of information."

Wassil and Lidiya could hear Dr. Kuzma's screaming voice. Lidiya smiled.

"Now. Now. Doctor. I would mind my language if I were you, if not for me, then for the sake of your daughter and her significant other."

There was more screaming.

The Major grabbed Lidiya's hair and twisted it, pulling clumps from her skull. He held the cell in front of her face.

Lidiya's scream pierced the silence of the room. "Father," she managed, "don't lis..."

The Major withdrew the phone while the adjunct placed his gloved hand over Lidiya's mouth.

"Doctor, I will allow you to speak with her if you calm your voice, and she hers."

He nodded to the adjunct to slowly release his hand from Lidiya's mouth, then let the quiet sink in before returning the cell to his ear.

"That's better. Now hold on."

He looked at Lidiya and gave her a thumbs up.

"I want you to tell him what we need," the Major said to Lidiya, "and please, nothing funny." He grabbed Wassil by the throat. "Or, I will make this man's life miserable."

The Major held the phone closer to Lidiya.

"Doctor Kuzma, he said, "I've put the phone on speaker."

"Father?"

"Lidiya, are you okay?"

"I am. These pigs ..."

The Major nodded to the adjunct, who slapped Wassil across the face. The sound was loud, exactly what the Major wanted.

"These men have a demand," she repeated, resisting the temptation to move closer Wassil.

"Nice," the Major whispered to her.

"I know," the Doctor replied, "and I've already told them I do not have an answer."

"And they tell us that if you do not provide an answer, my Wassil will be harmed."

"Your Wassil?"

"He is my partner," she replied, "and that is not important now. I am to be next."

"Okay, I will see what I can do."

"Thank you, father."

The Doctor had forgotten he was on speaker. "And Lidiya, surely that man understands that the prisoners move with the battlefield."

"I'm sure he does."

"Then ask him for some time for me to investigate."

"I will."

Lidiya nodded at the Major.

The Major brought the phone closer to his mouth. "Doctor," he said, "you have twenty minutes."

22

BOYKA

"You should leave the pub van behind," the Bucha soldier had told Nina. "We will see it put to proper use."

Nina found herself alone in a reclaimed BTR-80 remembering the horrors suffered by the soldiers on her first trip.

"My poor Fedor," she whimpered, her hand in her pocket, feeling for her crucifix, zeroing in on jagged edges of the missing footrest. "I know you were only trying to help."

Nina pulled the crucifix from her pocket and stared at the intricacies of the body depicted on it. "You have seen too much already, and you know what it is like." In her moment of desperation, she prayed. "So, I beseech you. Please, no more fighting."

The prayer didn't work.

Shots came from the left of the vehicle. Nina heard the familiar thud of the bullets but feared worse.

"Where are we?" She yelled to the driver.

"We are approaching Zhytomyr," responded a man shouting into the cabin. All Nina could see was his lower half, dressed in brown battle fatigues. Her eye was drawn to his knife. It hung from his belt next to a small, bedazzled crucifix.

"We appear to have run into some opposition," he said. "Hold on."

"I need to get out," Nina panicked.

"Shut the hell up and hold on, I said!" The driver screamed into the cab.

The BTR-80 pulled into a tight right, then an immediate left. The sound of bullets striking the vehicle stopped.

"We're going to run for it," shouted the driver, reassuring this time. "I'll have you out of this mess in a few minutes."

The driver was true to his word. After a few bumps and hairpin turns, the BTR-80 stopped. The driver got out and tapped a signal on the door of a warehouse to whoever was inside. Nina could hear a garage door opening, as the driver reentered to bring the vehicle inside. "There you go, Madam," the driver said, opening the side door. "We've arrived at a safe place, or I think it is safe."

"Thank you." Her appreciation sounded like something you'd hear an aristocrat say to their chauffeur. "I apologize, son. What is your name?"

"Andrii, madam."

"It is a wonderful name."

"Then it is sad you cannot thank my parents. They were the ones who gave it to me. Political thugs have taken them from me."

"Is that why you have that small crucifix hanging from your belt – to remember?" Nina pointed at the cross. "It appears to have lost its foot bars."

Andrii looked to his crucifix.

"There are no foot bars on this crucifix," he explained. " I am Catholic. My mother told me to say my rosary every day. I cannot do that, so I keep this on my belt in her memory."

"Andrii. Andrii." A stocky man called from an office in the facility. Nina did not have time to express her sympathies.

Andrii moved toward the man but kept his attention on Nina. "And Madam, I apologize for yelling at you in the vehicle. Politeness tends to evaporate when there is a threat of death."

"It is okay," Nina responded.

❊

Andrii's meeting lasted mere minutes. He, a stocky man, and six others emerged from the office, suited for combat. Unintelligible orders were bandied about as the group rushed out the back entrance. Two struggled to pick up large packs with long tubes. Each was labelled Stugna-P.

Moments later, Nina found herself alone in the facility. She thrust her hands into her pant pockets, feeling for the crucifix.

"I see what you did," she held it in front of her. "No more fighting for me, but not for them."

"Or I," came a woman's voice from behind her.

"Oh, I did not see you there. Who are you?" Nina spoke to a woman dressed in baggy slacks, a deep blue sweater and water-proof shoes. She looked to be Nina's age.

"I am the custodian of this facility. I keep it organized and clean so these people can do their jobs." The woman took a moment to scan Nina. "And speaking of which, you look like you could use a serious cleaning and a change of clothes."

Nina dropped her head to take in her blood-spattered cloth-ing. She lifted her right foot to better inspect her boot.

"I'll bet that boot is heavy given the blood it has absorbed. My dear, I fear you have been through traumatic times."

Nina stood silent, defeated.

"Wait here," the woman said before disappearing into a room in the warehouse. She reappeared a few moments later with directions to a makeshift shower and a pile of clean military clothes.

"A few weeks back, we were a larger group," she shouted to Nina in the shower, "but we have lost a few souls to evil."

"I see."

There was another moment of silence between them as Nina scrubbed the dirt and blood from her body.

"I could not help but see you are with a cross," the woman shouted. "Would you like time to pray after you are cleaned up?"

"No, the cross is more of a keepsake. I will be fine."

"Then can I get you a coffee and a sandwich?"

"Yes," Nina shouted back. She appreciated the offer and a chance to converse with a woman her age.

Nina finished her shower, dressed in the provided clothing, and then stepped into the slightly better warehouse lighting.

"Green with dusty grey and yellow tones," she announced to the woman.

"Yes, it is the M14 pattern Ukraine adopted a few years back. It's a pretty rugged uniform, and as you will note, there is a pant pocket large enough for your cross."

"I've already put it in there," Nina smiled. "And thank you for the waterproof shoes. I see they are the same as yours."

The woman handed Nina a coffee. "I am Boyka, by the way, and this is my home."

"I am Nina, and Shlisselburg is my home. I am here to retrieve my son. He's been unwillingly conscripted into this war."

Boyka skipped the opportunity for unproductive sarcasm. "Russian, eh?" Boyka replied with her brows dug deep in a pensive stare. "Your story sounds a bit far-fetched."

"I know, and I've had difficulty conveying it to both sides. All I can say is I must get Wassil back. This war is bullshit, and I will not allow myself to be a part of it, nor my son. There has already been too much harm."

"Well said, my dear. And, so I am clear, Wassil is your son?"

"He is."

"Where do you expect to find him?"

"Rivne has been suggested."

"That is two hours from here."

"I know. But then I need to find the prison my Wassil is being held in."

"That will be difficult since we do not know ourselves."

"Then my only chance is to be treated as a prisoner. How do you process your prisoners?"

"So far, I've seen them interrogated until they can give nothing of value. After that, the prisoners are either exchanged or handed over to Andrii. He takes them to a designated rendezvous point, and from there, they are sent to prison."

"The same Andrii who drove this vehicle," Nina replied with a quick nod to the BTR-80."

"The same."

"He knows where the prisoners are kept?"

"No, only the point where they are transferred to someone who does. It's an elaborate sequence, and I've probably spoken too much already."

"You have nothing to worry about," Nina assured her.

"I know because Andrii would give nothing up to anyone. He has already gone through extreme torture at the hands of the Russians. He didn't talk then, and he will not talk now."

"Except, know this. I want to go to where the prisoners are held because my son will likely be there."

"Then you will have to await his return. You just saw him running out the door to engage the Z Soldiers."

"Z Soldiers?"

"You have not heard of them?"

"No."

"They are Ukrainians who support Russia in their invasion. They are responsible for much of what you see outside."

"I see," Nina replied.

Both went silent as shots rang out from somewhere in the city.

"That will be them engaging the Z Soldiers now. I hear this kind of stuff every day."

"Then I am sorry for you and sorry the powers have put you through this."

A large explosion followed.

"That will be someone using the Stugna-P to decimate a tank."

"Boyka, you have a discriminating knowledge of battle sounds."

"What else can I do while I clean and organize, which brings me to this moment. What can you and I do while waiting for everyone to return safely?"

"Including Andrii?"

"Including Andrii," Boyka reassured.

"Talk?" Nina replied.

23

ANDRII

Nina enjoyed her conversation, during which Boyka listened for pops and bangs to identify the distinctive sounds of battle ordinance. On one occasion, there was a single shot.

"That comes from a sniper's rifle," Boyka declared.

Another shot rang out.

"That's the same sniper."

"How do you know?"

"The shot came from the same place," Boyka explained. "By now, the other side expects a sniper, so you will soon hear them retaliate with a barrage of small arms gunfire."

Nina didn't have to wait long.

"And there you have it."

Another sound soon overshadowed the small arms exchange.

"What was that explosion?" Nina asked.

"It's from a Russian-made F1 hand grenade. The blast from one of those scares me the most because grenades are anti-personnel devices. They rip through flesh with indiscriminate ferocity. It also tells me the fighting is in close quarters."

It was time for Boyka to move away from her identification lessons.

"What will you do when you find Wassil?" She asked, trying to ignore the battle sounds.

"I will take him home."

"And you think that a safe thing to do."

"It is where his home is."

"And you think the Russian politicos will let you be?"

"Why wouldn't they?"

"You will have helped a soldier desert. You will be executed for treason."

"Oh, I think I will be fine."

"I would not be too sure about that. Deserters and protesters are already being hunted."

"That is probably your side's propaganda."

"It is not. That information comes from your own battle-field soldiers. They are transmitting operational instructions on unsecured frequencies. We hear their conversations and news reports from their homes."

Boyka moved her chair closer as if to reveal a secret. "Nina, my dear, there is panic in their ranks. It is a panic well recognized by the state, and because of this, all retreats are seen as desertion. Citizen protests are treason. I'm afraid your side wants every hint of opposition eliminated."

"I am on no side."

"My apologies. But, let us say that we are looking at a return to the Stalin days of full-service totalitarianism."

"Full service?"

"Yes, where the state uses the military to arbitrarily arrest, deport or execute citizens they see as threats to their power. Dissent is crushed by fear."

"Fear?"

"Yes. 'You must not cross us!' That is their message, their warning."

"And that's as opposed to self-service?"

"Oh, yes. Liberal states do not need a military to keep people in fear, though most have them. Some endow their citizens with easy access to guns and constrain admission to education and health care services. People are subject to the arbitrariness of psychopaths, conspiracy thinking and indiscriminate disease. Those states call it freedom, but it only keeps people stupid, sick and in a state of constant anxiety."

"In other words, one prods the other neglects?"

'That about sums it up," Boyka nodded.

"And I suppose there is a better system?"

"There is no perfect system, and even if there were, I don't know what I'd call it. There is a hint, though, in some states. My research tells me social democracies fare much better than the totalitarianisms I just described. They are systems that see their people as thriving citizens rather than potential usurpers."

"Boyka, I must ask. Are you a political scientist?"

"No. I, like you, am a mother trying to keep her children out of the line of fire."

"What does that mean?"

There was no opportunity to dig deeper. Neither Nina nor Boyka had noticed the quiet until it was interrupted.

"Shhhh," Boyka whispered. "I hear footsteps."

"Your people are returning?"

"Not necessarily. Those footsteps could be our people. They could be the Z-people. They might be both, in which case it will be important to sort out who is in control. We won't know until that door opens."

"So we wait?"

"No! Come with me. We will take cover behind the office."

Nina followed Boyka through a hidden door into what looked like a panic room. A small video monitor revealed the facility's interior, focussing on the door. Nina could see her crucifix sitting on a chair next to the one she sat in.

Boyka took hold of Nina's wrist and gave it a squeeze. "Now, hold tight. We need to see who comes in."

Nina saw the door open, and the stocky man entered.

"Good, that's them," Nina sighed.

"Not so fast. That's just Marko. Let's make sure the rest show, either alone or with prisoners."

"You think of everything."

"You cannot be too careful," Boyka replied while tracing her index finger to count the arriving soldiers.

"*Dermo*, we have eight. We need nine!" Boyka let her hand drop to her side.

"Who is missing?"

"Andrii!"

24

A NEW PRISONER

"Now, where were we?" The Major asked. "Oh, yes. It is time to call your father again."

He no sooner got the words out when a group of soldiers arrived from the salon's back entrance.

Wassil and Lidiya stared wide-eyed at the group shoving a prisoner.

"Pay them no mind," the Major said as if he expected their arrival. "The sad-looking man is one of yours, and his life is about to get rough, rougher than yours."

The man was thrown to the floor in front of a sofa opposite Wassil and Lidiya. His face had been badly smashed. Every few seconds, he would let out a cough over his rapid breathing.

"That man's lung has collapsed," Lidiya said. "He needs help."

"He'll be fine. The sooner we get this done, the sooner someone will be able to look after him."

"But he needs attention now."

"No," the Major snapped at Lidiya. "Now, let us begin, shall we? And if it helps, we'll leave this fellow here – as long as his moans don't get too loud. Besides, he will be a great reminder for you to work fast."

The Major nodded at his adjunct, who dialled the number.

"I have him on the line for you, Sir," the adjunct replied after a few rings.

"Good," the Major said, extending his hand.

"Doctor Kuzma. I trust you have what we need?"

Wassil and Lidiya could hear a faint voice on the phone.

"That is too bad. Then I will pass you on to your daughter and see if she can do better. Oh, and one more thing, we have a third hostage. You are now putting three people's lives at risk."

The Major armed the phone's speaker and held it close to Lidiya.

"Father?"

"Lidiya? Are you okay?"

"I am."

"Get on with it," the Major shouted.

"Father, they need to know where the prisoners are kept."

"I do not know."

Doctor Kuzma's sentence was punctuated by the explosion of a pistol. Andrii's body went limp in the entrails of his own head.

The shot rang in the confines of the salon, deafening Wassil and Lidiya. Lidiya screamed. Both froze in shock.

"Well, look at that," the Major sneered after everyone had a chance to recover from the noise. "Turns out this man won't have a rougher time than you after all."

"You are disgusting," Wassil spat back. The adjunct retaliated by slapping him across the face with the back of his hand.

"Now, Doctor, let's try this again," the Major ordered. "Where are the prisoners kept?"

"Please, father, tell them, or Wassil will be next."

"I am telling you the truth," the Doctor said to anyone who could hear the speakerphone. "But I have something for you that might help. There is a man in Zhytomyr, where you are located. His name is Andrii. He is in charge of the prisoners."

"Well, that's a start. Where do I find this, Andrii?"

"By our last accounts, he is there with you."

"He is not."

"Our people report that he has been taken prisoner by the Z scourge and taken to the town square."

The Major looked at the body on the floor, then Wassil and Lidiya. "You have tricked me." He got up and cocked the pistol, pointing it at Wassil's head. "Now, it will cost you."

The Major was about to pull the trigger when a question occurred.

"How did you know where the prisoner was located?"

"You told us. Actually, you keep telling us. Many of your transmissions are on unsecured lines. It is easy to track you to a salon."

"Very clever of you, Doctor."

"No, very un-clever of you, Sir."

The Major's face reddened with rage. He levelled his pistol at Wassil's head and pulled back the hammer.

He never fired the shot. Instead, he fell back as a sniper's expanding bullet evaporated his chest.

The soldiers in the room fled through the back door. The adjunct scrambled for a defensive position near the showroom window. It wasn't good enough. A second shot fired through the Z-Soldiers gathered in front of the building, brought him to the floor. The soldiers outside gave up their defensive positions. Instead, they randomly returned fire while moving through the salon and out the rear entrance. They ignored their prisoners, but Wassil noticed the F-1 grenade in the hand of the last soldier.

"Quick, flat to the floor," Wassil yelled to Lidiya. He could hear the F-1 dropping to the ground outside the exit.

A moment later, an explosion ripped through the door and

supporting beams. Pieces of shrapnel embedded themselves in the walls and furniture. The blast's shock loosened dust and debris. Slabs of plaster and concrete at the back of the building collapsed, blocking the rear exit.

It took time for the crumbling to stop. More time was needed to allow the dust to settle.

Wassil was the first to stir. At first, he thought all was well until he felt for his leg. A grenade fragment had punctured his calf. When he tried moving, a pain raced through his leg. It was something he could not ignore.

Wassil then crawled to Lidiya to make sure she was all right.

She looked at Wassil. "You are hurt."

"It's nothing serious."

"Then let me see."

Wassil repositioned himself, and Lidiya examined the wound as best she could.

"At least it's superficial," she declared while steadying his leg with her hands. Lidiya then bit down on the fragment and gave it a tug.

Wassil let loose with a howl, then looked at Lidiya.

"That was very Hollywood," he said to her.

"No big deal, but you will need to stay off the leg, especially since it will be difficult to patch until we are untied."

"Which is what we will work on now."

"Then what?" Lidiya smiled.

Wassil lifted his head to inspect the room damage.

"We leave the way we came."

25

REUNION

"What happened," Boyka asked as she and Nina emerged from the panic room.

"We found them, or rather, Andrii found them," Marko replied.

"It's more like they found him," another soldier quipped.

"That's true," Marko acknowledged. "He's been captured."

"What?" Nina responded.

"Yes, Andrii spotted a sniper and drew his second shot away from us. The good news is that it allowed us to take up a position and destroy a troop carrier."

Marko looked over his shoulder at the man who fired the Stugna-P. "Good shooting, Artem."

"Anyway, those bastards aren't going to get too far."

"Any idea how Andrii is doing?" Boyka asked.

"How the hell would I know?" Marko snapped, his head bent to the floor, his hands on his knees. "I wasn't invited by those bastards to check on him."

"All right, gentlemen," Boyka declared, desperate to avoid a conflict. "What do you say we take it easy?"

"Apologies, Boyka," replied Marko. "We are under considerable stress."

"I understand," she replied, "and my question was instinctive rather than logical. I should have known better."

A red light flashed from the facility's ceiling, ending the apologies. It indicated an incoming radio transmission in the office.

"Jesus, already!" Another soldier cursed. "Won't they leave us alone for a rest at least?"

"Excuse me," Marko said. "I must get this."

Boyka, Nina and the rest of the soldiers stared through the office window, watching Marko engaged in an intense discussion. It ended abruptly with him slamming the microphone into its harness. He emerged with a long rifle in his hand.

"No time for rest, people," he declared. "We need to move. Andrii's been taken to a blown-out salon in Koroleva Square. We are to rescue him."

"I'm going too," Nina volunteered.

"No, you are not."

"But I must speak with Andrii. He is my only hope of getting in touch with my son."

Nina decided to borrow her old lie. "Besides, I could provide medical assistance."

"I appreciate what you're saying, madam, but you are not going."

"Artem," Marko said to Stugna-P shooter, "this could be a sniper's job, so take this 308 and use it well."

He handed his rifle to the soldier and then joined the rest as they scrambled out the rear of the building. When the door finally shut, Nina sprang into action. She grabbed her crucifix and stuffed it in her pocket before making for the exit.

"Where are you going?" Asked Boyka.

"To the salon," Nina replied.

"Do you know where it is?"

"No, but if I'm quick, your people will lead me there."

"Nina, you are a fool."

"Boyka, you are not the first to say that."

"Good luck, sister. I will listen for and mourn your death."

❈

Nina slipped out the back, looking for signs of the soldiers. None were to be seen.

"What now?"

She remembered how Boyka listened for the battle elements and realized the sound was loud enough to drown out parts of their conversation.

"The Square can't be that far," she figured. "I just need to listen for gunfire."

It would not be necessary. Nina glimpsed one of the soldiers giving up his rearguard position to move forward.

"That must be the direction I need to travel in."

Nina flanked the soldiers to the west and scaled several debris mounds before arriving at a position with a clear view of the Square. One of the buildings had a group of men milling around.

"Z-Soldiers," she thought, "this must be the salon."

She looked around the Square for her soldiers.

"They are well hidden," she thought.

All was quiet except for some yelling in the salon. Nina could not make out what they were saying.

Little seemed to be happening until a shot rang out, followed by a second.

The milling Z-Soldiers responded not by taking a defensive position in front of the salon. Instead, they fired wildly toward the sniper, then ran into the salon.

"They are trying to get away," one of her people shouted.

An explosion followed, and Nina saw the back of the salon collapse.

"Dear Jesus," she gasped.

Her soldiers revealed themselves as they flanked the building to cut off the Z-Soldiers.

This was her cue.

"Poor Andrii," she thought. "He must be terrified or dead. I must check."

She inched her way closer to the salon, periodically eyeing the area around her for signs of hostiles. She pressed herself against the wall when she arrived, then inched closer to the window. A quick peek inside revealed nothing.

Nina made her way to the other side of the window, then put her body into pushing the front door. It gave way with a complaint. She thought she heard a sound from within the room and backed off, returning to the window. Nina risked a second peek. The noise appeared to have come from the floor in front of a couch.

"This could be Andrii," she thought.

She returned to the door, this time emboldened. "There are no soldiers in here," she thought. "They are on the run."

Nina stepped through and into the showroom to see two corpses. They reminded her of Fedor and the pub van driver, and she was overcome with sadness and revulsion.

"Mother?"

The word didn't register at first.

"Mother!" This time with intensity and a familiar voice.

"Wassil?"

"What are you doing here? You are supposed to be home, safe."

"I've come for you."

"Jesus, mother, this is bad.

26

INTRODUCTIONS

In normal circumstances, Nina's impulse would have been to hug her son, like when Wassil returned from summer camp or when he came home on his first furlough. Sometimes a pinch on the cheek was included, which always embarrassed him. How she wished this could be one of those moments.

But, no. This time Wassil was haggard and bound, lying on the floor next to some woman.

"My Wassil," she cried, bending to hug him as best she could. "I thought I would never find you."

"Mother, I am happy to see you too, but right now, I need you to do me a favour."

Nina stood to await her son's instructions, but her attention was hijacked by the full extent of her surroundings. She saw Wassil next to two dead bodies. There had been plenty of corpses over the past few days, but this image filled her heart with profound dread.

Nina reached for her crucifix, squeezing it in her pocket.

"I hoped you would intervene rather than choose death," she said to the icon.

Her index finger glanced over the missing part of the footrest, bringing her dead husband to mind.

"Is this what you chose for him?" She asked, rubbing her finger along the jagged edges of the icon. "And for what? My sins? Our country? It was not I who broke the footrest off your crucifix. It was the devil's representative. It was evil, the evil you have come to represent."

She returned her gaze to the bodies before her.

"And here you are again trying to kick off the second footrest. I will not allow it. This time, I swear I will not allow it."

"Mother. I need you to pay attention."

"Sorry," Nina responded, her son's voice drawing her from her darkness. "I am overwhelmed. I only want to tell you how happy I am that we are finally together."

"And I too, but that will have to wait. Right now, I need you to free us."

"Us?"

"Mother, this is Lidiya. She is a prisoner here too."

"Of course."

"Lidiya, this is my mother. Her name is Nina."

"I am pleased to meet you," Lidiya answered with the awkwardness of a bride meeting an in-law for the first time.

"And, I, you," Nina responded.

"I wish this moment could be more joyous," Wassil interjected, "but we need to get out."

"Agreed," Lidiya acknowledged.

"Mother," Wassil pointed, "do you see the knife on the soldier's belt?"

"Yes."

"Get it, please, and cut these ties."

Nina was repulsed by the idea of getting close to a man whose head she could not make out. She approached slowly and lifted the corner of his jacket with her pointer finger and

thumb. Slowly the hilt came into view. So too did a small crucifix. Nina dropped the coat and started to hyperventilate.

"Mother, are you okay?"

"This man," she gasped. "His name is Andrii. He saved me
from a Z-Soldier ambush."

"That is sad, mother, but I need you to overlook your feel-
ings for him. Please pass me his knife."

Nina moved slowly. Like the child in Bucha, she laid her
hand on his corpse and let tears roll down her cheek.

"Mother!" Wassil yelled. "Get the damn knife."

The uncharacteristic harshness of her son's voice snapped
her out of her grief and revulsion.

Nina did as instructed, slowly easing the jacket to reveal the
knife, keeping her eyes fixed away from Andrii. She slowly
drew the blade from its sheath.

Nina cut Wassil free. He took the knife from her to attend to
Lidiya. Wassil lingered over her to clean the dust from her
clothing and sit her upright against the sofa.

"Thank you, Wassil," Lidiya said.

The extra attention was not lost on Nina.

"Great," Wassil declared. "Now, we need to get away from
here."

"To where?"

"West," Wassil replied. "To Poland. To Germany. Any place
but here."

"Simple enough in theory," Lidiya added, "but it is a long
trip. How do you propose we get there?"

"I agree, and walking is impossible." Wassil looked at his
leg, then gestured at Lidiya's.

Nina looked puzzled.

Wassil noticed.

"Mother, I have sustained a small wound which will make
walking difficult. More important though, Lidiya cannot walk at
all."

"I see." Nina paused a second. "Then we need a car or van."

Wassil remembered the motorcycle.

"I have a bike."

"For three?"

"I think we can make it work in the short term. I just need to get it."

He hobbled to the doorway. "Wait here!" He took a moment to look into the eyes of the two women who meant the most to him, two women who did not know each other. "And be careful."

27

SNIPER

The bittersweetness of the reunion gave way to the mission at hand. "I think this is the right direction," Wassil said to himself like a shopper trying to remember where they had parked their car.

"Ah, we meet again," he said to the bike owner's corpse. "And now I will fulfill my promise to you."

Wassil felt a slight pain lifting his leg over the seat. Fortunately, the bike started on the first turn. He twisted and turned it between the wrecks with minor effort until he reached the Salon door.

"Good," he said just before a single shot grazed the thigh on his already injured leg. Wassil dropped to the ground with the bike on top of him. A second shot followed with the bullet travelling through the bike's upholstery.

"Wassil." He heard his mother's scream.

"Get down, mother, and do not move. I will be there presently."

Nina did not respond fast enough.

A third shot cracked from the same position, this one nicking the top of her shoulder.

Nina dropped to the floor.

"Nina, are you all right?" Lidiya shouted.

"I'm fine. The fool tore the top of my uniform, and wait, yes, there's a bit of blood. Otherwise, it's just a scratch."

"Who is shooting at us," Lidiya followed up.

"I have no idea," Nina answered before Wassil could. "More important, what happened to our soldiers?"

"They're off chasing Z-Soldiers," Wassil confirmed after glancing along the Salon. "This one has managed to take up a position behind our people."

"Lidiya," Wassil shouted, "tell me you are okay!"

"I am," Lidiya replied, "and Nina, you are sure you're okay too?"

"I am dear."

Wassil gripped the bike's bars and lifted it enough to free his legs. One moved painfully, but both moved freely.

"Sheesh," he thought, "a collection of superficial wounds."

Another shot hit the brick of the salon wall.

It was Wassil's cue. He rolled to the entrance, then half stood, half leapt into the foyer. It happened before the shooter could get off another shot.

From there, he made his way to the showroom.

Nina was lying face down in glass in front of the showroom window, an easy target for another bullet. Blood had soaked the fabric of her shirt.

"Mother, I'm going to get you out of there."

"I'm ready when you are."

Wassil grabbed Nina's ankles and readied himself to pull her out of the shooter's line of sight.

"Now, mother, try and lift your head off the floor."

"Why?"

"So you don't cut your face."

Nina moaned but stayed clear of the shattered glass. Shards

stuck into her uniform, but none pierced her skin. "Boyka is right. This uniform is quite durable."

Wassil gave his mother a quick check, then turned to Lidiya. "Are you okay," he asked.

"I am. So far, no shots have managed to make their way this far."

"Good. For now, stay put," Wassil said.

Wassil went to the back of the ruined salon to retrieve one of the towels scattered on the floor. On the way back, he picked up the dead adjunct's firearm, an AK-47.

"Here, mother. Put this cloth against your wound and press as hard as you can. We want the wound to clot as soon as possible."

While she did that, he returned to the doorway to discharge a random burst of bullets into the Square.

"There, that should delay their attack if there's one."

"Their attack?" Nina asked. "It sounds like only one."

"Mother, I think you are right," Wassil responded.

"Son, I have been taught battle sounds by the best."

"Okay, then let's think this through." Wassil sat on the floor with his back to the wall. "The bike outside is our only way out if we want to create distance between the shooter and us."

"We only need a way to distract him," Lidiya said.

"Or I must hunt him," Wassil added.

"That would be too dangerous," Nina and Lidiya said simultaneously.

"And an alternative?"

"The distraction!" Again, both women spoke in unison.

"Then distraction it is, but what distraction?"

"Perhaps you could make the shooter think someone else is in the Square."

"Yes. I could try and move to another part of the Square. Then I could fire a few shots from that direction. That might distract the shooter long enough for me to return and get us on the bike."

"The distraction would have to be long enough for you to return and for us to mount the bike, which begs the question. How do you get three damaged people on a motorcycle?"

"One problem at a time, please. There is no time to waste."

Wassil started for the salon entrance, stopping short to look at the two women.

"Look after each other, please."

"Go," came the response in unison.

✻

Wassil fired another burst hoping it would cause the shooter to take cover. It must have worked because there was a pause before returning fire. By the time the shooter did, Wassil had rounded the salon corner. He made his way to the back and scanned his surroundings. Satisfied there were no hostiles, Wassil rounded two buildings and then cut toward the Square. He made his way through the debris and settled on a set of stairs next to a statue of SP Korolev to look for clues to the sniper's location.

Nothing.

"You need to get in closer," he whispered to himself.

Wassil inched his way around more wrecks, heading in the direction of the salon. At one point, Wassil saw a slight movement in the rubble, followed by another shot being fired.

"Oh Jesus, I hope that was not fatal." The thought of it made him angry, and he picked up his pace.

Wassil made his way close enough to make out the shape of a person lying between two vehicle wrecks. The shooter's rifle sported a scope.

"What kind of person knowingly seeks out and shoots a defenceless woman?" Wassil asked himself.

He inched closer, quicker this time and reckless enough to catch the shooter's attention. The shooter lifted himself and his rifle in a flurry of debris before facing Wassil.

The movement startled Wassil, robbing him of the reaction time needed to raise his gun first.

"Stop right there," the sniper screamed at Wassil.

"Okay, easy," Wassil responded.

"Now, drop your rifle."

Wassil took his time, half squatting to set it down beside him.

"Good! Now kick it away."

Wassil complied, asking, "Do you not know you are firing on harmless women?"

"I am avenging the deaths of the Major and his adjunct."

Wassil could see the man was injured, with blood caking his forehead and a stream blood running into his aiming eye.

"By killing civilians? That's not revenge; that's cowardly and cruel. If it's revenge you want, then I am your target. In the meantime, let these women be."

It was the only thing Wassil could think to say. He hoped the Ukrainians could return soon enough to take Lidiya and his mother away.

"Oh, don't you worry, I will. You're as good as dead."

The sniper raised his rifle and pointed it directly at Wassil's head.

"And, one more thing." Wassil interrupted the sniper's cruel intention. "What is with the Z on your collar?"

"Does it matter?" The sniper replied, half lowering his rifle to look at the badge.

28

HOW TO USE A PISTOL

"I never thought there would be a day when I would be crawling for protection." Nina inched her way to Lidiya to see if she was all right.

"I am fine," Lidiya responded, signalling Nina to stop.

"And you cannot walk?" Nina ignored her.

"That is true. I don't know what happened, but my legs refuse to move."

"Okay, as much as this displeases me, we sit tight until Wassil returns."

This was Nina's second time waiting, except this time, all was quiet, and Wassil was involved.

"You know," she volunteered to take her mind off her son, "there is always one thing to do when waiting through a battle."

"Oh," Lidiya said.

"Yes, my little one. We can listen for clues in the individual battle sounds. They give us a better sense of a battle's scope. When we have time, I will tell you about Boyka, the woman who taught me this skill."

"That would be nice."

There was a long silence between the women, during which Nina stared into the face of the dead Major.

"Of course, teaching it works well as long as you are not distracted by the morbidity of a corpse."

Lidiya half-smiled.

Nina focussed on the man's blue eyes, then gradually connecting the colour to her son's. She shivered as a wave of anxiety washed over her.

"What sort of man do you think he was?" Nina shook her head to rid of the feeling.

"A psychopath!" Lidiya answered immediately. "That animal was prepared to torture your son and me, kill us if he had to, just to find out where our prisoners were being held."

"Ah, I was trying to find Wassil too, though without the torture."

"And now you have found him. I am sorry it had to be under these conditions."

"It is not your fault, Lidiya." It was the first time Nina said her name. It felt natural – as if it had to be. "This man is to blame."

Conversational distractions would no longer redirect her from her anxiety – anger would.

Nina scanned the Major's corpse again, noticing a pistol on his side.

"I think I will take this," Nina said.

"Do you know how to use it," Lidiya asked?

"How hard can it be?"

"Just in case, let me show you."

Nina eased the gun from the Major's holster then handed it to Lidiya.

"This is a Tokarev pistol," Lidiya said, "used mainly by Russian officers. She checked the magazine for bullets and cocked the hammer. Then, more critically, she emphasized how to unlock the weapon and adjust its tricky safety.

"There you go." Lidiya handed the gun back to Nina. "It is loaded and ready to go."

"Mind if I give it a try?"

"What, fire it?"

"No. Go through the same routine you just demonstrated."

"Be my guest."

Nina repeated Lidiya's actions perfectly.

"Nice job," Lidiya declared.

"Thank you because this might come in handy."

Nina scanned the gun in her hand, then glanced at the Major before lifting her face to Lidiya.

"In fact, it might be handy now."

"Nina. Don't be foolish."

"Lidiya, my dear, I have come for my son, and some random shooter will not stop that from happening."

"But ..."

"Oh, and one more thing, that will be the last time you call me foolish." Nina smiled at Lidiya.

With that, she went to the salon door to peek outside. It was enough to get the attention of the sniper. He let fly with another shot, the bullet embedding itself in the salon's brick. The sound gave Nina a sense of where the shot came from. She veered in the opposite direction, behind another wreck, then another. Every move brought her closer to the Square's centre.

"By now, he will be wondering what is going on and intensely alert to his surroundings," Nina thought.

Every wreck, every heap of rubble, every remnant of a blast made her advance slow. She had no idea how close the shooter was until she heard sounds – the rustle of activity and a hostile conversation. She could make out Wassil's voice.

"I am too late," Nina thought. She panicked, recklessly moving closer to the words. She rounded the wreck of a burned-out bus and saw the shooter. He had his rifle pointed at a specific target as if getting ready to shoot. Wassil was hidden from her view.

Nina raised her pistol to the shooter and pulled the trigger. Nothing happened.

"Damn, I forgot to cock it."

For a moment, she stood mesmerized at the scene before her, waiting for the gun's barrel to flash, signalling the end of her son's life.

Then the unexpected happened. The shooter half-lowered his rifle, giving Nina time to cock the pistol and get off a shot.

She got the routine right and the shot delivered accurately.

29

A SHORT WALK

"Wassil?" Nina shoved the pistol into her pant pocket and moved toward his voice.

"Mother!" Wassil started to sprint in her direction. "Ouch," he complained after his first step.

Nina heard. "You okay?"

"I'm fine. Wait there. I'll be right over."

Wassil stepped past the shooter into his mother's line of sight. Her shirt was filthy, punctured by shards of glass and a blood-stained tear. Her look saddened and impressed. Wassil limped over to hug his hero.

"Ugh," Nina complained in their embrace.

"I'm so sorry, Mother." Wassil let go and took a step back. "You know you shouldn't be out here, right?"

"Wassil, so far, the only things you've told me are things I shouldn't be doing."

Wassil smiled. "And, by the way, great shot. You saved my life."

"That's better," Nina winked.

"Then, after you." Wassil extended his arm to escort his mother through the Square.

Nina did not follow. Instead, she pointed behind her son. "And what about this dead person?"

"His life is over, and his comrades will put him to rest."

"Rest?" Nina let loose with a short guffaw. She looked at the person she had just shot and then glanced back at the salon. "What an odd word! We both know that when the family of these dead people hear about their loved one's demises, they will not put them to rest. Their rage and sorrow will begin new hate narratives. Memorials will become recruiting events, and recruitments will become invitations to more death. These people will never be at rest. They will live on to feed my guilt and stoke their angry stories."

"You, and they, might forgive."

"I suppose."

"Look, Mother, we'll have time to reflect on this later. For now, let's get out of here."

Nina lingered. "I do not know you," she whispered toward the corpse, "yet I will always know you as the man whose life I took." This time it did not occur to her to rub her hand on his body.

❀

"Lidiya," Nina called once they were close to the salon.

"Yes?"

"I'm back with my son, our Wassil."

Wassil smiled.

"Now, we can focus on getting out of here," Lidiya replied.

Nina stopped at the entrance. "And is this the bike you propose for us to use?"

"It is."

"Too small! And too bad it didn't have a sidecar."

"Yes," Wassil replied in a defensive voice, "but not impossible for us to use."

He propped the bike between the debris of two vehicles.

"See," he pointed out, "it will stay supported. Normally I would get on first and stabilize it with my feet, but Lidiya will need help."

He returned to the showroom.

"We are ready to go now, Lidiya."

"And I am ready."

Wassil gently lifted Lidiya, then brought her to the bike.

"Mother," Wassil waved his hand to the opposite side of the bike, "get over there and help me lift Lidiya's leg across."

Nina complied. Wassil set Lidiya in the middle position.

"How is that?"

"Perfect," Lidiya smiled.

"Great, now you, mother."

"I'm not getting on that thing."

"Why not?"

"Because we are not going far."

"Say again."

"I want to introduce you to Boyka. She's a short walk from here."

30

WE SHALL BECOME SOMETHING ELSE

Boyka let out a squeal when she saw Nina.

"I did not expect you to return."

"And I half-believed you. But things turned out different."

"And to your advantage."

Nina surveyed the warehouse. "Where are the soldiers?" She asked.

"Oh, they will be back soon. By my reckoning, our people have chased the Z-Soldiers from the area. Our people will need a well-deserved rest."

"I suppose you know about Andrii?"

"I assumed he had been killed," Boyka replied, reverently lowering her head. "It fills me with sadness."

Nina reached for her hand. It helped.

"And what about you," Boyka continued. "What will you do?"

"I would like to call Dr. Kuzma."

"In Kyiv?"

"The same."

"He is my father," Lidiya spoke out.

"Then it is a small world, indeed!" Boyka stood back to get a better look at Lidiya. "Yes, I see the resemblance."

"Can we call him now?" Nina asked.

"That can be arranged."

"Good, because I am no longer looking for a prison. I have what I came for."

Nina stepped aside to allow Boyka a better view of her company.

"Boyka, I would like you to meet my son, Wassil."

"Hello," Boyka nodded. "You have been the object of a mother's powerful love."

"I know," Wassil replied, a streak of red brightening his face in embarrassment.

"And you already know Lidiya Kuzma."

"Lidiya, you probably don't remember, but I met you when you were a child visiting your father at the hospital. He is a brave man, you know. He does so much to help people cope with this infernal war."

"I know."

"Which brings me to the purpose of my call," Nina interrupted. "Wassil and I cannot return to Russia. And being Russian will make it difficult to live here. We need to go elsewhere for safety's sake."

"Understood," Boyka replied.

"And if I may," Lidiya interjected. "I would like to be included in your elsewhere."

The silly, pleading smile on Wassil's face said it all.

"Lidiya, my dear, it goes without saying," Nina replied. "Is it okay with you, son?"

"You already know, Mother!"

"Before this turns into a sob fest, do you have a place in mind?" Boyka asked.

"Not as yet, though a place with a similar climate, like-minded people, and a revulsion for the arbitrariness of state encouraged violence would be nice. What I'm hoping for is a safe corridor to exit this country. I believe Doctor Kuzma might be able to do this using his connections with the medical supply line."

"Then follow me," Boyka acknowledged.

She entered the office and fired up the transmitter. Nina followed with Wassil carrying Lidiya behind.

After a few validation exchanges, Boyka handed the microphone to Nina.

"Doctor Kuzma?"

"Yes?"

"My name is Nina, and I am with my son and your daughter."

"Lidiya?"

"Yes."

"Let me speak with her."

"Of course."

Nina handed the microphone to Lidiya.

"Father?"

"Lidiya. I was worried about you. Are you okay?"

"I am. I've been rescued and am with our brothers and sisters and a new family."

"A new family?"

"It is a long story best reserved for when we meet again."

"Then what is it you will do now?"

I am hoping for your permission to leave Ukraine but let me pass you back to Nina. She will explain.

Nina repeated her wishes to Doctor Kuzma.

The doctor expressed his support for their emigration if it meant getting Lidiya safely out of his haggard country.

"Are you sure?" He asked Nina, giving her a chance to

reconsider. "If you leave, you might end up somewhere where you are welcomed, and you might grow to be a family, but you will not be Russian or Ukrainian. You will become something else."

"Then we will become something else."

31

DIFFERENT WARS

The soldiers returned – all of them. Nina busied herself helping Boyka tend to wounds and prepare meals while listening to accounts of fights and tactics. Most of the soldiers dozed off. Eventually, the rest took a moment of silence for Andrii before settling for a much-needed sleep.

Nina stayed up to walk around the warehouse. The overhead lights were the high-intensity type she remembered from her time in the Shlisselburg arena watching her son in bandy matches.

None of the lights were on today.

"They're probably tied to the main power grid, which was likely destroyed a few days back."

The generator-fed LEDs were doing a great job though they cast long shadows. Everything in the warehouse looked considerable, more menacing.

"We must not settle in a warehouse," Nina declared.

"And so you shan't," the voice behind her replied.

"Boyka! I didn't hear you coming."

"I couldn't sleep." Boyka walked alongside Nina. "It would

be nice to walk outside on an evening like this, but we know it isn't safe."

"Boyka, you and I think alike, and I would have enjoyed getting to know you more, but we are fighting different wars."

"Russian and Ukraine? We are not enemies."

"I like to think so too. Still, it saddens me to have to acknowledge the cruelty it takes for one person to convince its people they need to go abroad and kill their friends."

"I agree, but this does not matter between us. Nina, you and I will always be friends. You, however, are fighting a new battle. You need to carry on with your life and the lives of those young people with you."

"That is true. And what of you? Would you like to come with us?"

"Thank you, but my place is here in this war. These soldiers need me, and I will not let them down. I will do my best to protect them from those who would do us harm."

"You are brave," Nina said.

"And so are you, especially given what you've been through these past few days."

"Then it will be goodbye for us."

"Yes, it will," Boyka replied, "in a few hours."

"Few hours?"

"We'll need to bug out soon. This building is too large and conspicuous for the Russians not to take note of. Besides, there has been too much activity around here for them not to take action. Frankly, I expect a drone attack on it at any time."

"That doesn't make me feel good."

"And so it shouldn't. We are taking a big risk by letting these people sleep."

Nina looked back to the fully dressed soldiers scattered on cots, mattresses and pillows.

"I hoped to hear some news from Doctor Kuzma," Nina said, refocusing on Boyka.

"Believe me, the good doctor will do what he can, especially since his daughter is involved. You will need to trust him even though there is a chance you may not hear from him."

"Thank you, Boyka."

"Now, what do you say? Try and rest. I'll wake you when the soldiers are up."

Nina agreed under the growing roar of a helicopter.

"*Korva*, we need to move now," Boyka yelled as she ran toward the soldiers. Nina followed suit.

"Everyone, up!" Boyka shrilled. "Now!"

She did not pause to let her alert settle in.

"You know the routine. Moooove!" Her tone sounded like that of a drill sergeant.

Nina watched as three soldiers scrambled out the door while others moved to the office.

Boyka looked for Nina, waving her arm toward the building's panic room.

"In there. Now!"

Nina saw Marko and a few of his soldiers heading for the room.

Wassil was already picking Lidiya up and positioning her so he could move as fast as possible.

"You'll find a ladder leading to a hundred-meter tunnel," Boyka yelled after her. "Follow the soldiers. They will take you to a street that connects with the E40. It will take you to Rivne, then Lviv and Poland."

"Got it. I know you said this would be good bye but would you not come with us?" Nina asked.

"No my dear friend, I must follow the men outside. They will guide me to a new warehouse."

Nina hugged Boyka. "Look after them, will you?"

"And you too, dear friend."

Nina, Wassil and Lidiya made their way to the office,

quickly locating the ladder. A trap door on the floor was already opened. Wassil looked into it.

"Down here," one of the soldiers called up. "Pass her to me."

Wassil did as instructed, then paused before descending.

"Mother, you first."

"No, my little *lapooshychka*, you. I am right behind."

Wassil did not argue. In seconds they found themselves in a dank tunnel barely tall enough to stand in. The soldier who accepted Lidiya carried her partway before transferring her to Wassil.

"I wish I could do this on my own," Lidiya complained.

"It's okay," Wassil soothed her, "we're almost at the end."

32

A CAR

Nina hoped they might emerge on a backstreet with a waiting vehicle for their use.

"A bit presumptuous," she thought when she found herself in a house basement.

"Is everyone okay," Marko asked.

"All good here," someone called back, followed by several others.

"And our guests?"

Wassil touched Lidiya and his mother's hands. Both nodded that they were fine.

"Here too," he announced.

"Good, because it's going to get rough."

Marko's sentence was punctuated by a thunderous explosion.

"That's it for the warehouse," one of the soldiers reacted.

"Let's hope the others made it out okay."

Nina thought of Boyka, but only for a moment. There was much to do.

"You two, check upstairs," ordered Marko.

"Sir."

"Nina," he continued, "I have been asked to provide you with a vehicle, which I will gladly do if I can find one in one piece."

"That would be nice," Nina responded.

"We just have to wait for the soldiers upstairs to report back."

Nina could hear their footsteps above, scurrying from one room, pausing, then to another.

"While we're waiting, do you know where you are going?"

"Rivne used to be my destination," Nina responded, "but now I think we are looking to Poland.

"Then Rivne is still on your list."

Marko pulled a map from his back pocket and laid it out on a work table.

"You will need to drive past it on your way to Lviv. You can make your way from there to Poland and, if I understand things correctly, to any number of supporting countries."

The soldiers returned to report their observations.

"All clear upstairs, Sir. The street looks empty too. And gauging by the glow on the side-room curtains, I'd say our warehouse is burning intensely."

The soldier appeared to be awaiting dismissal but suddenly spoke as an afterthought.

"Oh, and there are no immediate signs of our comrades."

"And a vehicle?"

"Sorry, Sir. The ones in front of the house are demolished."

"Just great!"

Marko didn't linger on his frustration. He instructed everyone to move upstairs into the living room.

"Permission to look for a vehicle, Sir?" A too-young Ukraine volunteered.

"No. I have another plan," Marko replied. "But for now, we

must secure the perimeter. Make sure we are not about to be surprised by intruders."

He set about assigning a small squad and then sent them on their way.

"And don't wander too far."

Marko moved with them to the back door like a nervous parent, sending teenagers off to their first dance.

"Now," he turned his attention to Nina. "When you travel to Lviv, know that the road from here to there is dangerous. But, it's the nicest four lanes you'll ever travel."

"That is good to hear," Lidiya chimed in.

"Except, hunter drones and helicopters will be around, looking for any excuse to vaporize a target."

"I take it you know this area well?" Nina asked.

"More than well and starting from this spot." Marko pointed to the floor. "This is my house."

"I am so sorry, Marko. This must be hard."

"Madam, it takes a special kind of cruelty for some dictator to force a person to stand in their own home and already miss it."

"I know," Nina replied, patting Marko's shoulders.

"But I am okay," Marko said, shaking himself out of his dark reflection. "I have something for you. I was hoping to acquire a car outside, but that does not look possible. So I have an alternative."

"Oh?"

"Yes. In the garage, at the back. We are restoring a 1958 Del Ray we picked up from a Cuban seller. It's an amazing and rare vehicle, except in Cuba. So far, we've rebuilt its engine. The body was scheduled next. It's still in rough shape, but as I said, the engine runs fine. It's low on gas, so you'll have to scrounge."

"Thank you."

"Do you have recommendations regarding the route?"

"I do. You've got 500 Kilometers to cover in a big, conspicuous car, but I suggest you make it longer."

"Can't be more conspicuous than a British pub van," Nina boasted.

Everyone stared at her.

"Sorry," she said, noticing their strange looks. "It's a long story."

"Anyway," Marko continued, "take whatever back roads you can, especially the P77 to the P05. There's a bus station at Ostroh where these two roads meet. You'll see a gas station there. Ignore it. It will be dead. Turn into the parking lot across from it. There is a long building with a blue roof and extra-large garage doors. You can't miss it. It's a solitary building occupied by humourless people, but they know me. They will guide you to a fuel supply."

"Got it."

"And if you get lost, keep heading west – always west."

"We can do that," Wassil replied.

"Great! You'll know you're not heading west when you no longer see columns of people looking to escape this nightmare."

Nina and Wassil nodded in agreement.

"And one more thing," Marko said, gesturing them from the backdoor to a garage, "It's a big car, made when fuel range was scarcely an issue. So, conserve your gas. With luck, you will need only one complete refill."

"Thank you Marko," Nina replied. "I do have one more item to clean up before we leave."

"Oh?"

"Yes. Could I speak with the shooter you called Artem?"

Marko yelled for Artem over his shoulder. "Make it fast."

"Hello Artem. My name is Nina. I'm wondering if your mother's name is Katrina?"

"It is."

"And she is from Chernihiv and currently working as a field hospital nurse."

"She is."

"Then son, please call her. She is worried to death about you."

33

ROAD TRIP

A gash on the garage roof told a violent story.

"Oh no," Marko moaned while opening its doors. The bomb that hit the warehouse was powerful enough to send one of the high-intensity lights through the garage roof. Marko saw that it caught the car's rear bumper, partially prying it from the body.

"We'll need to get the light off the bumper," he said.

"Let me help," Wassil replied, setting Lidiya down inside the garage entrance.

"Will you be okay here?" He asked her.

"I will." She glanced her hand off his shoulder. "I'll keep an eye out for Z-Soldiers. Do what you must."

Wassil took the AK47 off his back and handed it to Nina before joining Marko to lift the light. It didn't budge.

"We need a lever."

"Right," Wassil said, already rummaging through the debris.

"How about this?" Wassil pulled a miners' scaling bar from under a workbench.

"Perfect."

"This is a convenient thing to have," Wassil commented.

"We used it when we dug the tunnel from the warehouse. It still comes in handy when navigating an engine onto motor mounts."

Marko located a portable jack and set it beside the car. Wassil positioned the bar on top with the end of the bar dug in under the light.

"What do you say we give this a try?"

The men stood beside each other to put their full weights on the bar.

"Go," Marko grunted.

The light did not budge.

"Again." This time there was a slight movement.

"One more time." The light lifted high enough for Wassil to stick his foot out and push.

Still, nothing was happening until Nina joined in, pushing the light with enough force to have it clear the bumper.

They let go together on the count of three, crashing the light to the floor in a plume of dust.

There was little time to celebrate.

Shots were fired close to the garage.

"Go," Marko ordered Nina and Wassil.

Wassil, in a panic, returned to the entrance in time to see Lidiya pointing to the end of the driveway.

"The shots are coming from over there."

Wassil poked his head out to get a better look.

He saw two of Marko's soldiers behind a concrete fence periodically raising their guns to fire at an advancing group of Z-Soldiers across the road.

One of them spotted Wassil and opened up.

Wassil retreated, collecting Lidiya and scrambling for cover deep in the garage.

"We might want to deal with these Z creeps first. They've got two of your people pinned down behind your fence."

"Leave that to me," Marko said. "Give me five minutes, then start this beast and hightail it."

"I can stay to fight."

"No, you had best get as far from here as possible – and don't argue about it."

"Fine," Wassil said.

He carried Lidiya to the back seat while his mother got into the driver's seat.

"Mother, I think it best if I drive."

"Not this time, son. I've got experience on these roads and with a three-speed, column transmission. Do you not realize how old this Del Ray is?"

"Good point."

"You keep that gun of yours trained on those people shooting at us."

Nina counted five minutes, started the vehicle, then slammed it into gear.

The car exited the driveway just as a Z-soldier was approaching from across the street. Nina swerved in a tight left to avoid him, but the jutting bumper caught him, tearing a gash across his lower thigh.

"It looks like the other Z-soldiers are engaged in a firefight with Marko's people," Wassil reported.

"Then he is a good, brave man, true to his word," Nina said.

She steadied the Del Ray on the street. A few shots were fired in their direction by a few Z-soldiers who noticed them.

Ten minutes later, they were in the clear.

34

OSTROH

"Lidiya, how are you doing back there?" Nina asked.

"I'm fine."

"That's good. So you know, we are on the E40 and should be in Rivne two hours after we take the recommended detour."

"That's nice," Lidiya responded.

"And how about you, son? How are you?"

"Mother, I'm in good shape."

"What about those leg wounds?"

"They are insignificant. What is more important is you. How is your shoulder?"

Nina hadn't thought of it. The bleeding had stopped hours ago, leaving her military shirt with a scarlet shoulder lapel.

"We should have a look at it as soon as we can. You don't need an infection."

"We all need to have our wounds looked at as soon as possible."

"True, mother."

"Right now, I'm concentrating on keeping this aged beast on the road."

Wassil let her drive in peace while he scanned the car's interior. "It is a good car," he said after landing his eyes on Lidiya sprawled and sleeping across the back seat.

"Yes, there is plenty of room. I can't believe the auto oligarchs once made cars this big."

"Speaking of which," Wassil interrupted, "we are low on fuel."

"I noticed too. We'll need to stop soon."

Nina had passed several closed gas stations. "I suspect there won't be much gas available in these parts."

"I believe it has been cut off completely," added Wassil.

"There is some good news, though. By my reckoning, I'd say we will be at the P77 turnoff soon."

A kilometre later, Nina navigated the Del Ray through a left turn, heading south on the P77.

Wassil's face scrunched in uncertainty. "Are we confident about heading south?"

"Marko said to turn left."

"He also said to keep moving west."

"I know. In this case, all we can do is assume Marko knows what he is talking about."

"So far, it looks like he's right. This route is much easier travelling," Wassil observed.

"Of course, it is," Nina said. "There are no people on the side of the road."

Ostroh turned out to be a hamlet-sized community with a burned-out gas station on the right. The parking lot was empty, and Nina guided the car to the blue-roofed building Marko had directed them to. She stopped the car on the right side of the lot.

"It looks to be abandoned."

"I'll check the place," Wassil volunteered.

"Be careful."

"Ugh?" stirred Lidiya. "What's going on. Are we there now?"

"No. We are in Ostroh looking for fuel."

Lidiya stirred enough to notice Wassil about to leave the car.

"Where are you going?"

"To check the area. If there is trouble, I want my mother prepared to leave immediately, with or without me. Got it?"

"There won't be a problem, son. Just get on with it." Nina replied.

❋

Wassil exited the Del Ray and reached for his AK47 before making a complete circle of the car to ensure it was holding together. He approached the building next, taking in any sound that might signal a problem. "This is easy," he thought. "Everything is dead quiet around here."

Wassil decided to scout its perimeter before knocking on the building's door. A tangled thistle growth on the right side of the building delayed his advance to the back.

"What's that?" He asked as he pulled the plant's white fuzz from his clothing. Anxiety swelled in him as he picked up his pace. It was faster to take a long way rather than return through the thistles. By the time Wassil rounded the front corner, he saw his mother waving him toward her with a joyous smile.

"Wassil, I think we will be okay now," she declared. "I've found friends."

35

PROFITEERS

Waiting for Wassil had been excruciating.

"Where is that boy," Nina demanded?

"He'll be along shortly," Lidiya reassured her.

Then came the noise, the distinctive sound of gravel crunching under the tires of a slow-moving vehicle, the gentle purr of its engine, the squeaking of its brakes, and finally, the clicking of gears to formalize its full stop.

Nina slid into her seat to avoid being seen when she saw a van pulling in. It stopped halfway, on the opposite side of the parking lot. She reached her right hand to feel for the pistol she had set on the seat.

"We've got company," she announced.

"Who is it?"

"Don't know. The van stopped in my blind spot." Nina twisted the Del Ray's mirror toward the vehicle. "Hang on. I'll take a look."

Gradually Nina straightened in her seat until the vehicle appeared in the mirror.

"What the hell? This is great!"

"What's great?" Lidiya demanded to know.

"You'll see."

Nina got out of the car empty-handed and took a few steps toward the British pub van. It was identical to the one she had travelled in from the field hospital to Bucha.

"Hello," she bellowed to them.

The van's passenger-side window lowered, and a man hollered. "Hello. It is good to see you."

"On a medical run, are you?"

As an afterthought, Nina raised her index finger. "Just a minute, I'll get my son."

She turned in time to see Wassil rounding the corner of the building. "Wassil, I think we will be okay now," she declared. "I've found friends."

Wassil's abrupt stop had an alarming effect.

"It's okay. These people provide medical supplies for the Kyiv field hospital. They might be able to help us with gas and medical supplies."

Rather than approach directly, Nina saw Wassil move away from the building. "What are you doing?"

The hesitance on his face amplified his fears.

"Why?" She asked, twisting to look back at the van.

Three people had emerged with rifles at the ready.

"What do you want?" One of them yelled. His face was scarred below his helmet. He wore a camouflaged tunic and cargo pants with the legs tucked into black waterproof boots. The two people standing behind him dressed identically.

"To move on." Nina realized Wassil had moved from the building to draw fire away from her.

"Then you will have to tell that man to lower his weapon."

"Now, don't be like that," Nina conjured a mother's assertiveness. "How about we all lower our weapons?"

"Then, starting with you!" The scarred man replied.

"Fine," Nina called to her son over her shoulder. "Wassil, lower your gun."

She could see the disappointment in her son's face as he faltered.

"Wassil, listen to your mother. I say lower your gun."

"Mother, I only hope you know what you're doing."

"Stay quiet, son, and let me handle this."

Nina returned her attention to the interlopers. "Now you," Nina stared directly into the eyes of the leader like a mother about to scold a child.

They complied, partially.

"You still haven't provided us with an adequate answer," the scarred man asked again. "What do you want?"

"We don't want anything. We need medical supplies."

"Doesn't everyone?"

Nina ignored the sarcasm. "We also need fuel."

"Again, doesn't everyone?"

"Okay, I see what you're doing," Nina answered. "I am not in the mood to play games. So, are you able to help us or not? If not, let us pass."

"Strong words coming from someone as small as you. But yes, we have business with you."

"That's better," Nina said.

"Ah, but it's not what you think."

"Look," Nina interrupted, "all we need is a bit of fuel, enough to take us to Lviv."

"Oh, we have the fuel."

"Then will you allow us some?"

"Yes, we have plenty for the car, but not for you."

"I don't understand."

"Lady, you are driving a vintage automobile, and I suspect it's worth a lot. In fact, I intend on finding out. So step out of the way."

"Mother," Wassil called from behind her. "These people are profiteers."

All three interlopers raised their guns, one pointing at Wassil, the other two at Nina.

"They've stolen the van and the medical contents inside. Their aim is to sell it all on the black market. All we've succeeded in doing here is unmasking piracy."

"By?"

"By providing something else of them to sell – Marko's old car."

Nina looked at the scarred man. "Look, we need a vehicle to get to our destination. So the car is not up for negotiation unless you give us the van in return."

"Then we have a problem," the scarred man snapped his rifle at Nina. "Or, rather, you have a problem."

He sauntered toward the Del Ray, sliding his rifle strap over his shoulder and tossing the gun to his back. "Oh, and please tell your son to put his hands up."

One of his soldiers stepped forward to make sure Wassil did as instructed.

"This beauty looks like she needs a bit of work," the scarred man said into the side of the car. "And it looks like the back window might be broken."

"I'm afraid not," a prone Lidiya replied through the opened window. She pointed Nina's pistol directly at the scarred man's head. "You're the one who is about to be broken."

Lydia had managed to maneuver her body to retrieve the pistol Nina had left on the front seat. She then cranked the back window open, allowing her a clean shot at whoever approached the car.

It was too late for the scarred man. "Now, isn't this a switch," he conceded.

"It is," Lidiya confirmed, "so tell your louts to drop their weapons."

The scarred man raised his head to the sky. "Comrades," he ordered in exasperation, "drop your weapons."

"Nina," Lidiya called out, "tell them to drop their weapons unless they want their leader harmed."

Nina walked to the second soldier to retrieve his rifle while Wassil did the same with the soldier near him.

"How are you doing out there?" Lidiya called from the back seat.

"We've got them." Nina kept her weapon trained on the scarred man.

"Great, then I'll let you take it from here."

"Aw, how polite of her," Nina said as she approached the scarred man. "Your rifle, please."

"Gently," Lidiya warned.

The scarred man complied.

"Now, over here," Nina pointed. "I want you gathered in the middle of the lot."

"What would you like me to do with these guns?" Wassil asked.

"Bring them to the van."

Nina took a moment to think through her next move.

"I want you men to lay on the ground, face down."

"You will leave us the car," the scarred man asked, looking to buy time.

"We will," Nina replied before getting Wassil's attention. "Son, is it possible to shoot a hole in the Del Ray gas tank without causing an explosion?"

"Mother, that's the kind of bullshit you see in Hollywood movies."

"Good, then put a hole in the tank, please. Just get Lidiya out first."

Nina watched Wassil sling his rifle over his shoulders and then let her eyes follow him to the car.

It was the opportunity the scarred man needed. When Wassil reached for the car door, he kicked his feet at Nina, bringing her to the ground. He grabbed the rifle from her and stood, training its muzzle at her head.

The move almost succeeded.

Lidiya took aim between the opening car door and Wassil, then pulled the trigger. Her shot struck the leader's leg, and he buckled in front of Nina.

Wassil swung away from Lidiya to train his rifle on the scarred man.

"Mother, take that gun away from him."

Nina retrieved the rifle. "Got it," she said, stepping back and keeping the gun trained on her prisoners.

Wassil resumed his earlier task, lifting Lidiya from the car and bringing her to the van. He took time to settle her into a cot at the back.

"Wait," the scarred man interjected from the ground. "You mean you can't walk?"

"Just figuring that out, are you?" Lidiya responded. "Now, I would suggest you pay attention to that lady."

"Great! Now that we have that settled, Wassil, take the shot," Nina asked him when he re-emerged.

Wassil fired a single bullet into the Del Ray's tank, and gas immediately began to pour out.

Nina stood motionless long enough for the entire tank to drain.

"And there you have it," Nina declared to the scarred man. "The car is now yours. It's too bad you won't be able to get far."

"You bitch."

"Now, now. Is that a way to speak to a woman? Especially one who is about to attend to your wound?"

36

THE LAST LEG

After bandaging the scarred man's leg, Nina, Lidiya and Wassil shifted to the new pub van. Nina returned it along the P05 toward the E40 – the Lviv road.

"We're just going to leave them there?" Wassil asked.

"Why not," Nina replied. "Someone will find them eventually, and hopefully, it will be the right people."

"I hope so," Wassil replied.

"Besides, this vehicle will be much more comfortable, especially for Lidiya."

"That is true," Wassil reached to give Lidiya's hand a squeeze.

"But right now? We're on our way to the border," Nina announced.

The monotony of the P05 drive gave Nina pause to reflect on her time in the first pub van. She thought of the drone attack, the driver's death, his blood oozing, and her insensitivity. She glanced down at her military shirt.

"I am the fortunate one," she whispered to herself."

"What's that?" Wassil asked.

"Oh, nothing. I am remembering the poor soul who died trying to get me across the Dnieper."

"Yes, what did happen there?"

"It's a long tale I'll share later. Right now, we need to figure out how we will get into Poland."

At the intersection of the P05 and E40, Nina spotted a group of Ukraine soldiers. She had Wassil report the whereabouts of the profiteers and hand over their rifles. There was a moment of tension as some of the soldiers eyed the van occupants. In the end they saw no harm in them and let them proceed.

Aside from this, the journey around Rivne, and past Dubno, Brody, and Busk, felt more like a vacation than Nina's trip through the war zone. Even getting turned around at the ruins of an old synagogue near Brody helped engage the group in a historical discussion. Everything felt familial, pleasant – except for speed.

Refugees hindered their progress. Traffic slowed. Nina frequently stopped to help someone in medical need. Wassil took time to engage the refugees in conversations.

"Too many roadside people fret about the state of their documentation," he reported to Nina and Lidiya, "and too many engage in senseless spats with their fellow travellers."

Humanitarian groups penetrated deep into their phalanx, providing food and medical services.

"We are in desperate need," one of the medical attendants revealed to Nina during a stop. "There are too many sick people, and we lose too many of our supplies to profiteers."

"This is where the scarred man and his privateers would have done most of their damage," Lidiya commented.

"And where do you suppose they would have sold their ill-gotten goods," Nina asked.

"The Russians are reportedly starving for medical support, so I suspect they would be their obvious clients."

"Makes sense."

"Then it is good that we are returning much of it to where it is needed most."

Nina figured their average speed since leaving Lviv topped at 5 km/hr. "Look at those people," she frequently commented, "they are walking faster than we are moving."

Nina and Wassil took turns driving, sleeping, and attending to Lidiya. Once across the Rakuv River, they encountered a mixture of farmland and woodlands.

"The only good thing about the slow traffic here," Wassil tried to inject some compensating humour, "is we can nip out to relieve ourselves behind a tree without losing our spot in line."

He regretted the comment immediately when he thought of Lidiya.

"I am so sorry," he apologized.

"It is fine, my dear," she replied. "You have provided the necessary means." Nina and Wassil had set up a makeshift washroom in the van and made other arrangements to help her in her ablutions.

Nina observed all of this and was proud of how they worked together. She beamed at how they looked beyond themselves to keep an eye on the refugees. They frequently insisted on stopping to help the sick and injured.

"What have you noticed most about these people," Wassil asked her at one point?

"The sadness in the women who have left their male partners behind to carry on their fight," she replied.

"It is too obvious, isn't it?" Wassil confirmed. "This is yet another thing we have had to adapt to."

Nina was never sure she was adapting to anything. Time spent in the days-long traffic lineup gave her too much time to reflect. She wallowed in nostalgia, frequently weeping over the silliest of memories.

"Mother, would you like me to drive for a while?"

"No, son, this gives me something to concentrate on."

But Nina missed the life that defined her as a citizen of Schisselburg, especially the things she had taken for granted. "What of the chamomile and leopard's bane I love? Would those flowers adorn the base of Peter's monument, the statue I contemptuously slandered when I left?" Nina could smell their yellow and white buds in her imagination. "And what of my dear shorebirds and pigeons? Will I ever see them again?" A small part of her hoped Peter's statue would look good in the community.

Nina shook off her nostalgia at the Polish border.

"Get ready, everyone," she alerted Wassil and Lidiya.

"Finally." Lidiya hoped to give her escorts some respite and maybe figure out what had happened to her legs.

"I wouldn't get too excited. We were speeding at five kilometres per hour. Now we're stopped. It looks like the traffic is piled at the checkpoint. We're still looking at a few hours before actually crossing."

Nina, Wassil and a prone Lidiya continued administering to the sick from the pub van. Most medical gauzes and bandages were used to attend to injured or ill travellers. By the time they neared the border checkpoint, only the trauma packs were in supply.

"We'll be able to redirect these to the people on the front," Nina said.

"That will be good, mother, but we've got to think about what we say to these people."

"I know," Nina replied.

"I was talking to someone who had been to the checkpoint. Apparently, it's called Medyka, and the reviews for the crossing are poor. The facility is small, and its people are overworked, unfriendly and stressed."

"Of course, they'd be unfriendly. Busy and small cannot help but produce unfriendliness."

"That is true," Lidiya responded.

"Our real issue will be getting two Russians across," Nina added.

"We can proclaim ourselves as political refugees seeking asylum," Wassil volunteered.

"But not too loud," Nina spoke the words in a hushed voice. "Our presence could invite retaliation."

"And we don't have papers," Wassil added.

"That could actually help us," Lidiya said. "We don't need papers. Some countries have established a no-questions air bridge to places of safety."

"So staying quiet might suit us best."

"Then let me do the talking," Lidiya said. "Put me in the front passenger seat."

"Are you sure. You might have a problem getting comfortable."

"Comfort is the least of my worries right now."

Wassil retrieved Lidiya, helping her sit up. She moaned.

"Are you sure you can do this?" He asked again.

"I'll be fine."

"Okay, but let me know the instant things get too uncomfortable." Wassil rolled down her window before getting into the back.

37

MEDYKA

A guard approached the van on the passenger side and spoke Ukrainian directly across the cab to Nina.

Crisis creates instant families.

Lidiya interrupted.

"Apologies, Sir, but my mother-in-law cannot speak. I can help you, though."

The guard ignored Lidiya. Instead, he craned his head to look into the back of the van.

"And you?" He asked, catching Wassil's eye. "Can you speak?"

"I can," Wassil replied, "but I'll let my wife do the talking."

"Not before we open the back first." He signalled two juniors to meet at the back of the van. Together they swung the door open.

"Now, while they inspect, I have a few questions."

Lidiya did not give the guard a chance to ask one. She opened, saying they would like to return the van to the proper authorities. "It can be restocked to continue its humanitarian efforts."

"How do we know you haven't stolen this vehicle?" The guard countered.

"If we stole it, why would we return it to a place where we would be caught?"

The guard paused to think about Lidiya's answer.

Lidiya began to feel uncomfortable. She rubbed her eyes. "Maybe I can wish this person away, she thought."

Nina reached over and touched her arm. It was the recharge she needed.

"Look," she interrupted the guard's pondering, "I encourage you to call Doctor Kuzma at the Kyiv field station. He will attest to the purpose of this vehicle."

The guard signalled another guard to meet with him away from the van. After a few inaudible words were exchanged, he returned.

"Stay here," he ordered.

The second guard lingered with his own questions.

"How was the trip from Lviv?"

"Slow, and with too many people suffering along the way," Wassil answered.

The guard turned his attention to Lidiya

"And you, my dear, what was your job in Ukraine?"

"I was a nurse with the military."

"So, you are deserting?"

"No. I am injured." Lidiya sounded offended.

The guard let a slight grimace escape his face.

"Oh, too bad, but you don't look injured to me."

"I cannot walk. My legs do not move."

"Really?"

The guard opened the door to take a better look at Lidiya.

"How do I know you are telling the truth?"

"You will have to take my word for it."

"Or, I could ask you to leave the van."

"You could, but I won't." Lidiya's contemptuous gaze penetrated deep into the guard's eyes. Within moments he averted his eyes. "Besides, I can't, not without help. And even then, I would not be able to stand."

"Then let me help you." The guard might have been bested in her argument, but he was not without malice. He grabbed Lidiya's arm, giving it a pull toward him.

"Keep your hands off her," Wassil yelled.

"Or what?" the guard asked.

Wassil heard the metal-on-leather rub of a sidearm withdrawing from one of the junior's holster. He pointed the gun directly at Wassil's head.

"Fine," the guard relented, "then let's approach this differently. I want you to step out of the van first."

"I've done nothing wrong," Wassil replied.

"I'll be the judge of that."

Wassil crossed his arms in defiance.

Nina forgot her culture. "Wassil," she ordered in Russian, "do as he says."

A second junior reached for his gun.

"Well, well," the guard grinned. "What do we have here? A Russian?"

"Two Russians," one of the juniors added.

"Shut up," the guard scolded the junior.

More juniors arrived. Two climbed into the back and began rummaging. It didn't take long for one to find Wassil's AK47 under a blanket. He had forgotten to return it to the Rivne soldiers.

"Okay, I want all of you out of this vehicle immediately," the guard ordered as two juniors carried Wassil out. "You are under arrest."

Nina was frustrated. "You do not understand. I am here to rescue my son from this infernal war."

"I'm sure you are," replied the guard as he again reached for Lidiya's arm.

Wassil reacted by breaking from his captors and running at the guard. He caught the man at the waist landing his total weight on his tailbone. Wassil lined himself up to deliver a follow-up punch.

Within moments the juniors had picked the guard up. Once upright, he shook them away.

"You'll regret doing that, Russian."

The guard steadied himself to deliver a punch.

"Hold him still," he ordered the juniors. Several attached themselves to Wassil's limbs.

"Oof." Wassil buckled under the first blow.

"Stop! Stop!" Nina and Lidiya screamed together.

Another punch was levelled but not delivered.

"Stop!" This time the word carried a commanding tone. "That's an order!"

The juniors stood down. Wassil dropped to the ground.

"My apologies. I am an officer with the Straż Graniczna. You are Lidiya Kuzma, I presume?"

"That is correct."

"And these two are Nina and Wassil?" The officer's limp gesture at Wassil acknowledged he was there without involving him in what was going on.

"Again, correct."

"Well, your father sends his greetings. He is a good man."

"How is he doing?"

"He loves and misses his daughter, as any father would in these circumstances. He understands you are seeking refuge abroad and wishes you well. He knows you are travelling with two Russians who are also seeking refuge. He asks only that you try and let him know where you have settled."

The officer ordered two juniors to escort Nina and Wassil to processing. Another was dispatched to retrieve a wheelchair.

"That ought to do it," he finalized. "I wish we could talk, but

I'm sure you can appreciate how difficult these times are here in Poland."

The officer took two steps toward his base before stopping.

"Oh, and for goodness sake, keep him up-to-date on children."

EPILOGUE

May 2037

There were no island views from her Brookside Avenue stoop. Instead, Nina looked along the rim of a mighty Precambrian basin peppered with pine stands and the roofs of houses peeking over their tops. It was a good thing there was no island since that would have reminded Nina of the Oreshek Fortress and caused her to lapse into memories of the Russian-Ukraine war.

"The only thing significant about any military artifact," she thought, "is its memory of misery and penchant for pain."

No, Canada was her new home now. There were forts here too, but she stayed away from them. Instead, she fixed on her new country's reputation for peacekeeping.

"That was my role in Ukraine," she beamed with pride. "If my country was unwilling to keep the peace, it was up to me, even if I had to fight for it."

"*Babushka?* Who are you talking to?" Keeva hopped up on the stoop and onto Nina's lap.

"Oh, no one, my dear. I'm just thinking about how it was

your mother, father, and I came to be here and how much I long for my old home."

"Oh?" Keeva replied while smoothing the hem of her dress across Nina's legs.

"Yes, and did you know I had friends there? I even remember their names. They were Olga, Emma, Arena, Galina, Natasha and Sasha. When I left my home, they were the last people I saw from my town."

"And you miss them?"

"I do, and I've meant to call them for years. I've just not had the nerve."

"Do you not think they have worried about you all these years?"

"I suppose so."

There was a long silence while Keeva fidgeted with the hem of her skirt.

"*Babushka?*" Keeva broke the silence. "When you were worried about my father, what did you do?"

"I went and got him."

"Then maybe it's time for you to get your friends. At least get in touch with them to bring them peace of mind."

A tear formed in Nina's eye. "My precious Keeva, you amaze me with your wisdom."

"It only makes sense to me."

"And yet your wisdom is more." Nina shifted her body in the chair, inviting Keeva to stand in front of her. She then held Keeva's shoulders and looked deep into her eyes. "My precious one, you helped me define a statement I once used when we were journeying here."

"Oh?"

"Yes, a wise doctor explained that I would become a part of something else when I moved from my homeland. I responded saying, 'then something else it is.'"

"Something else?"

"Yes, my question exactly. Would it be Russian or Ukrainian? Would it be Canadian?" Nina fought back a tear. "No, Keeva, you have taught me what that 'something else' is."

"What is it, *Babushka*?"

"Peaceful."

They hugged.

ACKNOWLEDGMENTS

Story ideas come from all around us, from our existences. The impetus to write the story usually comes from supportive friends.

Thank you to Dave Leblanc for an early discussion of the hero-mother idea. We both heard the news from Ukraine and how they would allow Russian prisoners of war to return home if their mothers came and got them.

Thank you to Carrie Latendresse, Bill Romas, Frank Fortin, and Spencer Chaput for reading the early drafts, ferreting out tiny errors, asking insightful questions, and making considered suggestions.

To Bob King and Rod Burns for the education on complicated motorcycle riding.

And above all, thank you to Gail, my wife of 46 years. She read and re-read the manuscript, recommending editorial changes to help make the story more readable.

ABOUT THE AUTHOR

Michael C Kelly is an author and award-winning educator. He lives in Sudbury, Ontario, Canada. Michael draws his ideas from his experiences as a bartender at a Royal Canadian Legion, a corporate cash management assistant, a regional economic development officer in Northern Ontario, a college professor, and a volunteer for various community organizations. His philosophy builds on the notion that the greatest gift one person can give to another is to pay attention to their existence.